Samuel R. Delany

Science Fiction Hall of Fame
SFWA Grand Master
Winner of the
Hugo Award
Nebula Award
Locus Award
Tiptree Award
World Fantasy Award
Shirley Jackson Award
Stonewall Award
Mythopoeic Fantasy Award

"I consider Delany not only one of the most important
science-fiction writers of the present generation, but a
fascinating writer in general who has invented a new style."
—Umberto Eco

"The Nevèrÿon series is a major and unclassifiable
achievement in contemporary American literature."
—Fredric R. Jameson

"The very best ever to come out of the science
fiction field. . . . A literary landmark."
—Theodore Sturgeon, on *Dhalgren*

R. Delany

PM PRESS OUTSPOKEN AUTHORS SERIES

PM PRESS OUTSPOKEN AUTHORS SERIES

THE ATHEIST IN THE ATTIC

plus

"Racism and Science Fiction"

and

"Discourse in an Older Sense"

Outspoken Interview

Samuel R. Delany

PM PRESS | 2018

"The Atheist in the Attic" was originally published in two parts in *Conjunctions*, 2016. This is its first complete appearance in book form.

"Racism and Science Fiction" was originally published in the *New York Review of Science Fiction*, no. 120 (August 1998), and first appeared in volume form in *Dark Matter: A Century of Speculative Fiction from the African Diaspora*, edited by Sheree R. Thomas (New York: Warner Books, 2000).

Series editor: Terry Bisson

ISBN: 978-1-62963-440-1
LCCN: 2017942914

Outsides: John Yates/Stealworks.com
Author photograph: Scott Dagostino
Insides: Jonathan Rowland

PM Press
P.O. Box 23912
Oakland, CA 94623
www.pmpress.org

10 9 8 7 6 5 4 3 2 1

Printed in the USA by the Employee Owners of Thomson-Shore in Dexter, Michigan
www.thomsonshore.com

CONTENTS

The Atheist in the Attic

"Philosophy is homesickness. It is the
desire to feel at home everywhere."
—Novalis (as cited in Thomas Carlyle's essay of 1829)

Shortly after I accepted employment with the duke, John Frederick, in November 1676, I, Gottfried Wilhelm Leibniz, arrived at the house of the Amsterdam acquaintance with whom I'd be staying for three weeks while performing legal offices for my patron. By the end of my second afternoon I had made a five-hour trip for a six-hour visit to Baruch Spinoza's home in The Hague (the first of three visits over three consecutive days). Back in my Amsterdam rooms, I thought over those hours. I was thirty when I wrote these reflections—wrote them rather too freely, I now suspect, given what has occurred since his death three months after our meeting, as well as over the last twenty-two years of my life. (Gunter and his sisters have divided themselves between Africa and the New World. Would you believe it from what I've written below? I wouldn't.) Since the death of Ernest Augustus and the ascension of George, I've reread it. But I don't think I shall rewrite it, since in two years the eighteenth century will open up about us—or enfold us in its chaos.

1.

There was nothing grand about *his* home, which almost all things here—the candelabra on the lace cloth at the ends of the downstairs dining table, the brass bar holding the carpet to the back of each broad step, the yellow blossoms brocaded on the wand of the bed warmer leaning by the fireplace in my bedroom suite—make me remember. (Though severity is in keeping with the nation, domestic Dutch decor is too austere.) In the few hours I've been back I've seen three servants: one man coming from a door at a second-floor corridor's end and (I glimpsed them over the banister) two women walking together across the front hall. They were carrying starched lace toward the dining room, as I was going up.

No Peytor yet, but apparently he was among the lowest in the house.

Gunter does not live opulently. He keeps a household staff here of only sixteen, for him and his three younger sisters—one of whose conversation and anecdotes about her travels I find more interesting than Gunter's; one of whom I find a lively talker about fashion and gossip, if the topic itself is a bit tedious for me; and none of whom is currently at home. From my last visit two years ago, I suspect all three girls find their younger brother a bore.

But aren't journals such as this basically occasions for candid assessments?

No. They're not. They're for telling oneself the fictions that are as honest as you can make them and still keep your life bearable.

Sixteen in *this* house is not quite one servant for every two rooms.

2.

There, of course, I'd seen only one—and would have been surprised were it more than two. The woman who'd answered the door turned out to be the landlord as well as the red-brick building's owner. An owner answering her own door? *That's* very Dutch. Or seems so to a German like me.

But I write this back at Gunter's.

Yesterday morning just before daybreak I took a cart up from the boat (I am so glad the duke owns his own yacht), with my three trunks containing eight pairs of pants, a dozen lace-fronted shirts—party and plain—jackets for everyday wear, enough wig powder to choke a full reception of young officers, my travel cloak, my greatcoat, my smallclothes—since baths are at a minimum I travel with lots of them, which makes me eccentric—my mechanical calculating machine (my own design, with just the fewest suggestions from the Hamburg horologist who constructed it last summer according to my seventeen pages of careful plans) stored with my books (some of mine for casual gifts, two of his I hope no one but he will know—while I'm here—I have) and papers in my luggage—and my calculus still in my head. That's where I want to keep it right now, ready for the upcoming attempt at friendship in England.

Moonlight and window light had flecked the broken canal. The three of us in the Duke's party staying in the city crossed on an early ferry. Horses huffed out breath and hoofed at cobbles, and the deepest blue emerged above the water and was reflected in it; nor was the air that cold.

And today I am back again—from my first visit.

Settling into my suite, where I'd slept a few hours and risen before three in the morning, I'm trying to make sense of the fragments of these last hours, these last days, this life, and the possible world that might sensibly hold both a here and a there.

Today was my first visit anywhere since I'd arrived, you see. Or, for accuracy, I could say it was my second. "One" is the easy fiction. "Two" is the slightly more embarrassing one that society, good manners, and expediency compel:

I did it.

It wasn't *that* important.

Let's leave it out.

I would have felt very bad if I hadn't at least thanked that young man back in Hamburg who'd cast his wheels and cogs, and bolted his cylinders to their metal rack, and his grown daughter of almost thirteen who'd polished them all, and his father who'd actually come in one day and made the two suggestions that allowed the whole thing—as I said above, or did I say it?—to work. Did I thank them? The uncertainty throws guilt over all my present actions. But experience says forget it—or write him a note apologizing for the oversight if it's still that disturbing. Writings that have come down to us from the classical Greeks suggest those bright people had a mail service of sorts. But most of the last thirty years in Germany, save in the larger cities, there has not been.

And I can imagine a third fiction that says: Oh, of *course*, modes of politeness are not important: They're not important the way garbage carts are not important. The way sewer pipes in cities are not important. (And Venice and Amsterdam have developed such different sewer systems from Paris—which practically doesn't have any—or from London, which does.) They're not important the way money that moves around the city and keeps buildings and byways, churches and bridges from falling to pieces through extravagance or bad judgment isn't important, or the peoples who have been forced by laws—and *our* laws, after all—largely to confine themselves to the management of financial loans in the greater mode of investments are not important. (They're not important unless you don't know them.) It's not important the way anything is "not important" that we leave out of fictions too quickly and glibly told. In short, what could be more pressing to articulate, to analyze, to carefully oversee than politeness—the thing we assume is so well understood, so widely shared, that it allows a simple "good morning," "good day," or "good evening" to make sense? Suppose our days were six months long, and our nights as well—as some claim is the case at the poles of our own great globe, which has grown so much larger in the last hundred years that whole counties can lose their postal systems for a century or so? What would happen to the most ordinary greetings on the street? What happens if there are no streets as such on which to greet each other . . . ? Is that a good enough reason to think that China and India, Africa and the Americas, whether at pole or equator, are simply uncivilized because they are different? Or that anyone from them, unto their greatest and most powerful rulers, is not worthy to clean up our shit? Really, such ponderings are absurd. At least I think they are. Sometimes.

And other times, they don't seem so.

Or take this in an entirely different direction: Does bringing such questions and assumptions to light mean you are a politically revolutionary genius, so that all you have to do is shout—in the proper place (that is, in the most improper place you can think of)—"birth!" "joy!" "sewer pipes!" "money!" "slaves, women, the poor!" "onanism!" "copulation!" "smallclothes!" "shit!" "pain!" or "death!"? Or that such improprieties might lead to a revolution for the benefit of the nation, the world (or poor women slaves)? In truth, I don't know. I must be mad. (Why did a great queen privilege an old, rude genius, who, twenty-six years ago, must have been at least ninety at her court . . . ? Everyone who's anyone today knows that's where he died. No one remembers that I passed through with my uncle when I was six—and I remember meeting him. And where shall I end my life, should my age suddenly and surprisingly treble? Some place where I shall be not more remembered there than I was then?) But a thank-you note might be a start.

3.

I'd arrived in Amsterdam planning to make *eight* visits, for all of which I already had letters of introduction from my duke and for most of which I had already written out personal notes to precede me. Only the first was I passionate about making, however. The others (which as of this evening still lie ahead) are to my patron—or to people my duke wishes to patronize.

As soon as my carriage had drawn up at Gunter's elegant grounds and town house, which I'd assumed would be my

Amsterdam home for the next twelve days (two weeks, shy one weekend for travel on to the next place that lies ahead, as does another visit tomorrow to The Hague), and today assume will be for the next eleven, I'd climbed down to the paving between the hedges (the driver had been paid back at the docks). Someone declared: "Oh, you're here! Wonderful. You can go on up if you want—if you're tired, of course." It was Gunter, outside my closed carriage, in his own open one. (I leaned forward to glimpse him through the window in my carriage door, in morning wig and afternoon coat.) "But I don't remember you *ever* being tired before two at Altdorf! I've given you three rooms on the third floor. Mary and Peytor will show you where you'll be—when we get back, you and I. It's the suite my uncle used to work in whenever he'd stay with us. He's been dead four years; we've hardly used them since. You remember Peytor, don't you? Well, he remembers you! He didn't stop talking for three weeks the last time you left us. About *you*, too. And as soon as he heard you were coming again, he asked could he please be assigned you while you were here." (Wondering what he was getting at, I opened the door, which was slightly loose and, starting to climb down, smiled and shrugged.) "You know me. I let them run me," Gunter went on, "really I do. I haven't got the personality to do this sort of thing properly. And don't even talk about the girls." (Perhaps an invitation of some sort that he was leading up to?) "My inability to manage a house is half the reason why I never married. You *could* spend a bit more time with your host, couldn't you?" He burbled on, while I tried to fathom *what* was behind all this chatter. "Look, let them get your things up there if you don't mind them unpacking for you— they do it for me, whenever I travel: I take them around with me;

certainly they can do it for you while you're here—you can look it over later." He sighed. "Peytor's not used to it." And Peytor . . . ? The truth is, right then, I had *no* idea whom Gunter meant. (Nor, since he meant a servant, was I particularly curious, right then, to know.) My last visit had been two years back, and Gunter had certainly never mentioned him in a letter. "But Mary will keep him in line. I don't know if you were aware of this—we rather rescued him from the country back in the summer of '72." He stopped, as if he'd remembered something. "My *dear* Gottfried, whom I haven't seen in ever so long, I have to"—he took a breath, and I realized he'd started in on a confession—"drive over to see an . . . an old Jew. There's nothing for it; there's no getting out of it. Oh, you know how that is. Come with me, and we can at least start catching up . . . ?"

So it *was* an invitation, and one he was embarrassed about, of course. (*My* dear *Gottfried, I have to take some money to a . . . a young woman. Oh, you know how it is.* I could hear him say it in the same tone of voice.) "I have a feeling I'm not going to see much more of you than when we were at school—and I don't want to think how long ago that is. You've written me how busy you'll be this trip." Leaning on his carriage edge, he smiled imploringly. "Come. At least I'll get a few moments with you." He really was perfectly happy to let his housekeeper assign half of his full complement of servants to devote themselves to my arrival so he could have another few minutes' talk with me before our day grew hectic. We are so selfish and squander so much at this social level where the fame and infamy that count are both invented.

"Certainly." It seemed rude not to. (Just as it would have were we visiting his paid mistress.) But I stood there a moment, between vehicles, feeling it would be unseemly as well to leap too quickly to fulfill my friend's awkward request. "You've always been a very generous friend to me," I said, wondering why he couldn't extend that generosity a bit more and leave me alone to arrive.

"And I always felt the time we did spend together," he offered as recompense, "was some of the most pleasant I've ever had with anyone."

Then he opened out his carriage door, and I climbed up. He stepped back for me, and I took a seat across from him. But such endless and minuscule anxieties as mine were the price, I reflected, of working so hard at—and sometimes even succeeding in—being a good houseguest.

While on the street, from the house, from the garden behind it, from the small maintenance building to one side of it, his people were calling to each other to busy themselves getting my things inside, we set off to pay his Dutch Jew a call, as if the world had offered an unexpected stutter to my own plans: my secret Jew tomorrow, presaged by Gunter's ordinary Jew today.

And, yes, I wanted it to be a secret—candidly.

I wasn't planning to make much of my visit the next morning, either to Gunter or to anyone else. No, I wasn't hiding it—exactly.

But when you are a busy guest of a busy host at a sprawling and busy home, sometimes you can disappear for a day or even two or three and not attract much attention, either before it happens or once it is over. (Right now I hope only this journal will know. And probably even it will have to be studied and reread generously to reveal its secrets and separate chaff and grain, gold and grit—assuming there's gold or grain to it at all. Also, at thirty, one is of an age to know how silly most such hopes are.) I have been wondering since the beginning if I ought to record it, or even if—now that it's occurred—I might be too excited to write about it.

True: So far I am not. (I feel just excited enough . . .)

But I remember, as I sat in Gunter's open carriage, more or less comfortably muffled (*was* it colder today?), listening to his chatter, and chattering back what seemed—when it seemed—appropriate, while we went off to see his Jew, if I should really be calling mine a Jew at all.

His own people no longer did. Did he? Today he signs his name Benedict instead of Baruch. I wonder if he's learned how little difference that makes in how anyone else talks of him—including me. Or if he cares.

And, of course, the always awkward third truth: this invitation to see another Jew this morning made me feel as if the world were mocking me, as if it were pushing me to say, even now: "You know I'm going to be seeing that Spinoza fellow tomorrow, if he'll receive me." And I was *not* going to say that to Gunter! I was not going to say it because I was protecting my own reputation. I was protecting Spinoza's as well.

And I was protecting Gunter's and his family's, I told myself, not to mention those strangers who'd already involved themselves in his case, those scattered in the Netherlands and Germany and France as well.

But wouldn't the world be a better place if I didn't have to?

(When your own reputation already entails a philosophy such as mine, serious thoughts about *preferable* alternatives can only make you weary.)

"Of course," I said, "let's go," just to plague myself with the discomfort of knowing I had decided—not to lie, exactly, but to withhold the truth, at least from Gunter. Or, at any rate, to delay his knowledge of it.

Till I have seen my Jew? Or till after I've left with my trunks and bags and notions of the world for another two-, five-, or ten-year hiatus in my friendship with Gunter. Would I tell him tonight or tomorrow? (No! That was insane! Would I tell him in a year, a decade, ever? How could I know?)

We drove in his carriage to the Jews' neighborhood, with more chat about his sisters, his servants—"Sophie will be particularly unhappy to have missed you"—his youngest sister—"as would Peytor if you'd come three months later—I'm giving him half a year off to go back to his family in Flanders and help them out." (What in the world is it about this Peytor?) "If he'd missed you, he'd never have forgiven himself or me, for settling his leave in winter instead of the spring—"

I asked, "Farming? His family?"

Gunter said, "Of course, that's what they do." He looked at me with the hint of questioning that asked, *What else could it be?*

And I wondered when (or if) I was going to see this young houseman. (Or was he an old one . . . ?) I had no memory of what this Peytor looked like. I assumed he was here on my last visit. But one meets so *many* servants in the course of the quasi-diplomatic circuits I am always moving through, I find myself not even trying to keep them in memory.

When we got there, Gunter gathered himself up. "Do you mind waiting out here? It's one of those matters . . ." Now *he* smiled, shrugged, even opened up his hands, as if—I fancied—to show me he held no weapon. "I'm sure you understand."

"Not at all." I smiled back.

Gunter raised his eyebrows. "Unless you'd like to come in just to get—?"

"Really." I shrugged scarf and coat. If anything, I was too warm. "No, really. I'm quite comfortable—at least now."

Once or twice the horses stepped about so that the driver had to still them. And I was rocked along through my thoughts in the carriage—which were, I'm afraid, little like the ones I've been writing here.

Above the door how many years ago had someone carved the Hebrew homily *emet veshalom yesod ha'olam*. Quietly I read it. It's supposed to be Jews speaking to other Jews. We gentiles (it assumes) merely overhear it and therefore trust them more. But couldn't it be Jews speaking to us as well, accusing us of making the world the mess that it is?

I wondered at the discomfort of sitting below its accusation: No, you really *are* lying to this generous man, your friend, a member of your nation and class, endangering him and his family, moreover endangering yourself by planning this secret visit, and still moreover endangering the man—the Jew—you claim so greatly to respect that you hardly dare to write such a vilified name even in a journal. (No, I *will* write it!) Spinoza may be the most peaceful man—or Jew—in the world, but the world that he lives in and that I live in is not. And not to talk about it is a blatant lie of omission.

Could that *shalom* (peace) if not the *emet* (truth) have been Jews scolding specifically the man I'd hoped to see the next day, the most peaceful of men by all reports by those who love him, and evil beyond all bearing by those who vilify him. Does the homily ask him: "Why have you fueled all this rage and uproar around our city, our country, our Lord's world, whether your people's Lord or mine . . . ?"

But apparently he'd been doing that through his whole life: wasn't that why his own people had already excommunicated him?

By the time Gunter came out again and walked from under the words I had been reading and rereading—the stone words over the door—feeling around under his cloak for his inner wallet, I had decided—truly, short of abandoning my plans to see him at all—that my actions and my reticence both were for the best. But I wondered why—still—we had to live in a world where that was the best we might have.

Better, the intaglio words were an absence of stone.

"Well"—Gunter stepped up to the carriage and pulled back the half door—"that wasn't as complicated as I was afraid it might be. I think he knows, in money matters, it's well to oblige the wealthy. And you're a good friend for your support. Really."

He climbed in. The driver shook his whip near the animal's ear. We started home.

Really, had this been necessary? But that, I thought, was my old friend.

4.

When we got back to Gunter's, my traveling trunks were no longer about the steps.

Gunter pushed inside, not ringing for anyone. A cool smell of dust in the cavernous front hall. Neither Peytor nor Mary was there to take me up to my room. "Come with me." No one at the front to take Gunter's coat or mine, either. He looked around, clearly put out, then shrugged grumpily and hung his over the banister. "Sixteen men and women," he said. (That, by the way, is how I first knew for sure what I've written above. Or maybe it's not important and I should cross this out—since clearly that's implied.) "And do you see a soul? I must have said it a dozen times in the last two months. Someone's supposed to be in charge of the door at *all* times. Leave yours there, too."

"It's all right, I'll take mine up with . . ."

But he already seemed to have forgotten. As we started up, a woman in a bonnet and Dutch apron came hurrying in from a door along the hallway with its flowered paper. "Oh, sir—I'm so sorry, I was just out at—"

Gunter loped up two steps, looked back, and declared: "We've gone through this before, Hilda. *That*"—he pointed to his coat on the rail—"best not be there when I come down. Come on, Gottfried. I'm afraid you're seeing us with our clothing all untied and unhooked. Are you sure you don't want to leave it?" Then, I realized, he thought better: I was a guest, and an eccentric one. "Let's go. Follow me and I'll show you where you are." Halfway up, of course, all of a sudden he remembered something he *had* to do. "Before eight thirty. Someone's coming, and I have to get to this—so we'll be ready. Really, we've been putting it off since . . ." He sucked his teeth. "Anyway, that's *why* I had to see the Jew. Look, you just go on up there. Turn . . . left; that's right, left; you're the end of the hall. I'm sure the suite's open. Mary would leave it unlocked, I know. Peytor—it's a toss-up with pretty much everything he does, till he does it a dozen times and gets his ear pinched a handful of times for doing it wrong. So it's a matter of who left last. Once you're up there, you can ring for someone to take your coat down if you'd like." And he hurried off over blue carpeting toward what I assumed was his own suite (though his working spaces were scattered though the manse, unless he was one of those gentlemen who try to work alone in concentrated isolation. It's surprising how little I knew my host, especially in these last years.)

I continued on, feeling as if every new piece of information just accused me further. Finally I pushed through my door.

It was a very nice room—the first of three. Mary and Peytor—or possibly just Mary with Peytor getting instructions from someone (Mary herself?) who could do it far faster than he (I assumed he didn't pay the most steadfast attention)—had fin-ished unpacking my things in the bedroom, behind the two sit-ting rooms. The shutters were opened. The drapes were back. The trunks themselves I went to see in the walk-in closet. I opened the one on the top: my writing equipment, my papers—and, in the trunk's corner, my mechanical calculator, bronze and bright, with all its parts turned by a crank that lay in the wooden box beside it. Wisely they'd known not to touch those.

I closed the trunk.

As I looked around, I thought: Someone has put some thinking into how this had best be done, so that I, the presumed beneficiary of that thinking, need not think at all. But here I am, thinking anyway about the individual thoughts such thinking comprised, approving this bit, questioning that one, disapproving of another—well, thinking about what's not supposed to require thinking, that *is* philosophy, no? (Wasn't this all predicated on how to get out of the house leaving as few signs as I could? "No, sir. His coat's gone from the downstairs closet.") And all creatures who can think must indulge it one way or the other, some more, some less, some better, some worse, all the way up to the Great and Terrible Gods of Men, wrangling and warring among our princes over the explanations offered for His behavior, and even unto your behavior in response to Him. My mind on the peaks of Zion and Olympus, Ararat and the Mount of Olives, I went to the dresser, opened the top drawer, and pulled it out—

Smallclothes. Mine. All of them.

I'd expected handkerchiefs, hose, and shirts in the top of the bureau.

This had to be Peytor. A sensible and experienced servant—like Mary—would either wait till asked, or, if he didn't know what they were, put them in a bottom drawer. At various grand homes where I'd been a guest, that's what had happened over the years.

No, this had to be a boy—and a boy who'd waited on me once and whom I couldn't remember. Mary, with whom I was equally unacquainted, would have thought differently—if I trusted Gunter's passing account.

At the desk in the middle room, I slid a visitor's card from my wallet and signed it.

I took out a sheet of paper, waiting for me in the stocked desk, dipped my quill in an ink bottle in its elaborate stand—it had been refilled, I assumed, within the hour—let it drip twice back into the inkwell, so that ink rippled like the sea (or one of the canals outside), then moved it from the left side of the paper, to the right side, to the left again, and again to the right, while I debated whether to write my note in Latin or Hebrew. I read Hebrew as well as any educated German once destined for the clergy (before the law had grabbed up all my energies), and I speak it tolerably. But my writing, that is, my Hebraic penmanship (unlike my Greek and Latin) is, frankly, dreadful.

I moved my quill to the left, to begin.

All right, Latin.

My esteemed colleague, Herr Spinoza . . .

And I explained how I had gotten his address from our mutual friend, Herr Oldenburg. I knew his health was not the best. I would be at his home in the vicinity of eight the following day. If he were not up to seeing me, he should merely decline to meet. I would respect that completely. But I was prepared to go the trouble of coming and risking his dismissal, as a sign of the great respect in which I held his learning and wisdom.

I signed it—

Your humble servant and fellow in truth, Gottfried Wilhelm Leibniz

—and added several titles, though I was sure he must know my work at least as well as I knew his. After all, he had written a book on Descartes. Presumably this would convey I was his equal or superior in society, though ready to learn from him if he would make the effort to teach me.

When I finished and waxed it and stamped it with my seal, I rang for someone to get it into the hands of a messenger. Ten minutes later when no one had come, I stood up, took my letter, went into the hall, and started down the stairs. Somewhere there *must* be servants in the house. Maybe now was the time to call on the good will of the curious Peytor. But I knew nothing of him. Was he fourteen? Was he twenty-four? And none too swift— which now that I'm thirty I know means something different when it is applied to the city poor or the city rich, the country rich or the country poor. Or even men and women whenever they occupy one or the other varied station. There was a ribbon on the table with which to tie the letter.

In the polishing room behind the pantry, three women worked at the old plank table with their kidskin and rouges and the silver candlesticks that may well have been the work of the same artisan who'd made the dining-room candelabra.

One paused, rubbed the bridge of her nose with her knuckle, and, when I asked for him, told me that Peytor was on loan to the stable of the house two east of here. Yes, she was Mary. But she could tell me where to find a messenger. Let her put down her work a minute—her soup spoons and rubbing cloth—get her winter shawl and wrap up against the afternoon damp and gray. Two other women were sitting on the far side of the room with pillows on their laps and half a dozen wooden bobbins hanging down them, weaving at their lace as if their lives depended on it, not even looking up when Mary came back.

Outside were a group of poor fellows. Mary walked me up to them, and they explained they would take a message anywhere locally; one said he'd even take letters to outlying townlets— Haarlem, Utrech, The Hague—because he had relatives who lived there and he could stay over if he had to, and while mail was dear, people were realizing more and more and more that it was worth it. Mary had three letters herself she wanted to start on their way. Though she would take no offence if mine were too important to send at the same time as a simple country woman's, getting gossip to her aunts and cousins—

"Oh, don't be silly, old woman," I said in Dutch.

I assume she shared my thirty years—though probably the powder I wore made me look older, like a city corpse ready for interment. The talc is supposed to keep you cool and ward off skin cancers if you spend any time outdoors in the country sun.

Our boys were sullen and with large hats down over their ears and whiskers; two were tied on with scarves. No, getting out to The Hague was a full day's ride. Yes, he (the one with relatives there) would have it there by evening. Then a city church announced noon. We agreed on a price that both Mary and I thought acceptable, though she looked dour. But I suspect that was her response to prices in general. Possibly she thought the whole idea of sending a letter by a paid messenger rather than waiting for a relative or a servant on their way in a wagon an unneeded extravagance.

And I hoped my official seven—two others in The Hague, one in Utrecht, the rest in Amsterdam itself—would not take such a tedious amount of time once I got this one out of the way.

I needed to get an early morning carriage for the next day and a driver. Which I managed to secure—again with Mary, since a diligence was at the corner. (I was not about to use Gunter's.) So when the mantel clock said three in the light of the lantern beside it, I was up, washed by a second lantern I'd lit from the other, and into new hose, doublet, and undercoat, from smallclothes to great coat.

I wore only a small wig.

Before the fine sand ran out in the candlelight, I grabbed up the baggy wallet with the books I'd wanted to take, looked in it (wrong wallet of course, so I went back and got the right one), snuffed the light and went down—and outside found my driver asleep under horse blankets up on the carriage bench. I was clothed for this time of year and of night, as Gunter had insisted when I'd mentioned to him I'd be getting an early start but not saying exactly to where.

And I was on my way south to The Hague.

5.

Sunrise was just breaking when I got down at his door (this morning). I told the carriage driver to go away and come back toward the afternoon—then stepped back a moment—

Had my letter preceded me, or had it arrived so late last night it could do no work at all?

I went to the door, then returned to the driver to ask him to drive around till sunrise was real—

But I looked up to see a lamp in a second-floor window behind shutters; the shutters opened, and a bundled figure called, "Excuse me? Did you want anything, stopping here like this?"

"No, no, of course not. But yesterday I sent a letter—" Next I knew, over my protests that it was much too early to want anything at all, the woman was pulling back the front door.

"Hello, again. Now come in, please. Please . . ."

To repeat myself, the house was not grand. From the edge of the street, looking up into the end of night, I could make out three stories.

Again I was about to call back to my driver to take himself off for a few hours, only to see him, on the carriage bench, tugging up those blankets as heavy as canvas over his own greatcoat and big Dutch hat, to lean down on his side and, I'm sure, go momently to sleep.

Practically at the same moment, the woman from upstairs opened the white door with its knocker I probably wouldn't have thought of using if I hadn't seen her light, and we said through the now-vertical crack, "Good morning." She went on, "I'm the landlord and owner here. Did you want to see someone . . . ?" As I've already said: How Dutch. And with a few more commonplace phrases, she and I mimicked conversation accurately enough, so that possibly we even communicated some meaning.

In her baggy white nightcap (not a servant's) and her woolly shoulders in their blue shawl, she ushered me into the hall. (How do you call that room and the one downstairs at Gunter's both by the same word . . . ? But if you didn't how could you communicate about anything?) "No, we got your card last evening. The first thing he said was, 'He's coming at seven or eight? I don't suppose there's any chance he'll be early—as five or six say, when I'm up and at my most alert. Well, it's only another visitor . . ." (The Dutchman? The Jew? The philosopher . . . ?) She brought me into a downstairs room with several severe, hard-backed chairs. "Let me go up and see what he says."

While I sat and waited, undoing my muffler—no closet that I could see, no cabinets either, nor even a sideboard, and the house (or the hall and at least this room) chill enough so that it seemed reasonable not to have taken my coat—I found myself wondering why I could not remember the name of the first Jew I had visited—though, true, I hadn't actually met him.

But, in Gunter's open carriage, I'd sat in front of his door, looking up at his incised lintel. Finally, a servant had come out to tell me they would be a few minutes more. Would I want to wait inside? Oh, thank you—though it was more for curiosity than need. I wasn't cold yet. We'd gone in, walking through to his back room—and heard him laughing with Gunter. And because the rather cluttered side room had its own back door ajar, I stepped out into a garden and waited under some surprisingly tall elms over a little table and spent my last three minutes staring up at a wooden lintel with no words on it at all.

Which only made me think more about the others out front.

Then the servant, Gunter, and Gunter's merchant host each joined with the other to apologize to me, while I said, no, no, no, I was fine.

In the carriage, both before and after the visit, Gunter had mentioned his Jew's name half a dozen times, and on the trip home even suggested I might be interested in his services and he would introduce me next time, but this time it had just seemed awkward. You know how that is . . . ? It was as if this other— Spinoza, not yet present—had driven the earlier one, now gone, irrevocably from my thoughts.

Driving to his house, Gunter had repeated it enough. But it hadn't been important . . .

I heard a creak, and looked up at the wall. It came from the stairs in the hall. Then, he in his dressing gown, the woman pushed open the door for him and walked him in. He leaned on her. (It was that time of year when, if there was no fire, you kept the doors of the rooms closed, at least in a house of such low station.) "You're visiting our city?" he asked in Latin, as he came forward. "Will you stay long?" As I looked around that bare room, with some pitchers on the table, a basket in the corner, red tiles on the floor, and a crucifix (I could not imagine it his, but it might have been his landlord's—unless it was to put people off), I felt—if only from the speed at which he moved to the topic of my leaving—he was actually to be a bit of a bore. (Momentarily I remembered Gunter.) Or, at any rate, he had a strange or low notion of politeness. That was not how the refined Descartes had met one at an evening soiree, those old enough to know him said. *Hello, there. Hope you like our city. When are you leaving it . . . ?* I mean, really. You can say that and make it sound funny. Or you can say it and make it sound ignorant. But it's most disturbing when you hear it and can find no signs of what thoughts lie behind it, or what thoughts don't.

6.

Perhaps, twenty-five years ago, a much younger Spinoza had attended a few of Descartes's talks in the city with a list of questions to ask (so I'd heard from Ollendorf); and during the thirties when the Frenchman had been a resident of Amsterdam, the Jew had written his book. Yes, years back, as a child I'd glimpsed Descartes in his last year in the Stockholm court. No, I could not call him a friend in the way the very young may sometimes be befriended by the old. But I did not have to call him stranger . . . at least in my circle.

"Why have you come to see me?" They were not his first words. Still, I wondered if they'd prove happier than a few exchanges of meaningless small talk. Are important questions rendered meaningless because we are not prepared—he, I; teacher, student—for an answer?

The woman moved a chair nearer to him, then stepped away. "I was going to bring you up to him. But he said, because it was you, he really wanted to come down . . ." And to the frail man in his robe: "Are you all right, now? Can you take care of yourself?" She looked at me. "If he gets tired, just call upstairs. I can hear pretty much everything."

"Why have I come to see you?" I repeated in Hebrew (with such a man, with or without small talk, I assumed honesty was best). "Because with a small amount of work, you have created in me an extraordinary need to . . . to know you."

"True"—he chuckled—"I never thought of myself as overly prolific," he answered, still in Latin. Then: "I write letters, there's my treatise on Descartes, which I've given some of my friends in manuscript, my Hebrew grammar—" Accepting my offer of respect, he now spoke to me in Hebrew. "I didn't think I had written enough of anything to influence anyone very deeply."

I reached into my wallet and took out the book—which I'd had my binder put between leather covers more than a year ago—and held it out. He reached forward and took it from me, opened it; then, seeing what it was, smiled.

He raised it a little, leaned down over it. "My Descartes study. My first attempt to write publishable Latin."

"*Principia philosophiae cartesianae.*"

"Yes, my first book." He looked up again, smiling. "At the time I was afraid it was going to be my last, too. I'm surprised you have it." (I read his expression as one of having been pleased he'd made a right choice about the language in which we would hold our interview.) "I only wish my eyes were good enough to reread the text. Right now, I'm putting together two works. There's the one that grows directly out of this one—the same method, the same rigor, that deals with my own poor ideas of how the world might work. Then I'm doing something I've always wanted to do, and will perhaps finish once I've finished the other—"

"Is that your Hebrew grammar? Some of the friends to whom you'd sent copies have showed me one or another of the earlier chapters. I found it fascinating. I think that's because if you read any textbook three times, even in a language you don't know at all, at the end of the third time through, it's surprising how much you will have picked up. Was that your experience as a child?"

He nodded. "Yes, it was."

I went on. "Your Hebrew grammar will be a very good grammar book indeed. Much better than the one I used as a boy, aspiring to wisdom and tradition. It's clarity and thoroughness are impressive." I'd put my wallet on the floor against my high-heeled shoe.

"I'm still surprised you read it."

"Why would I not? We are educated men, you and I. I know you know this as well as I do. You read a textbook to learn the topic. But you also read it to learn of the teacher. My tutors considered me a prize student in all three—Latin, Greek, and

Hebrew. I think it's a talent that goes along with a love of philosophy. I expect it will for a long time—at least I hope so."

"I studied Hebrew from the time I was three. And got my prizes, yes. But I didn't take up Latin till I was sixteen—and on the other side of the city, too. The Gentile side." He said it ambiguously, as if it were a meaningless distinction, an inaccurate designation. Then he looked sternly at the book he held (it had my name on the cover, since I was the one who'd had it bound). "Sometimes I wonder if my Latin is up to the tasks I've taken on with it."

"Your Latin," I told him, "is quite eloquent for the tasks you've taken on. It's muscular, direct, with the virtues of the republican writers rather than the later decadents . . ." I smiled. "My Latin tutor, and my Greek tutor, and my Hebrew tutor, all three—all five, actually—said I seemed to have a knack for languages. For a few years, they were all the same man. Then they were all different men and several of them at that. Then one again—"

"At my Hebrew school, I had two for all the years I attended. But we could not study Greek or Latin. It was only when I was fourteen that I realized, from what I'd learned of the world, that I was on my way to being an idiot. So, two years later, I got up the nerve to travel halfway across the city and learn Latin from a generous Dutchman who wanted to bring the world of culture and thought to anyone and everyone who wanted it, poor, Jewish, foreign and unfortunate, energetic or lazy, who thought it might be good to brush up or simply had managed not to learn Latin at all. I remember that study well, now. The old Roman republican writers, once I began to acquire some vocabulary, were the easiest to read. The decadents and euphuists are hard. And I've been told more than once my style is rather crabbed."

"Your style is easy," I said, "for one who knows the language. Your thinking is exact and very much your own. But such thinking always has its difficulty—for anyone."

"How much of my grammar have you seen?"

"Two chapters," I said. "Oldenburg, our friend at the Royal Society across the channel, showed me a section."

"To be honest, I'd rather know what you thought of my old study of Descartes than what you thought of my grammar book. You said you read it."

"Twice. Parts of it many more times. Clearly Descartes was a man you admired, as do I. When I'd read your highly logical opening comments, I recognized what your final comments went on to confirm with even more rigor and richness than I'd been expecting. Your Descartes was my Descartes. We *want* to know intelligent people we agree with. We want to find out if we will agree with them about more things than we do already. In that sense, you gave me what I wanted, and even more of it than I felt I had any right to expect."

"I'm going to sit here," he said, got up, moved over, and lowered himself slowly to another hard-backed chair. On his knee, covered with his robe, he closed and opened, closed and opened his hand. "If one looks more comfortable to you, please, take it. Please."

I was in a larger, softer chair. "Are you sure you wouldn't prefer this one?"

"No." He sat straight, not letting himself lean back. (The same bore, I thought, who wanted to know when I was leaving.)

"This one is easier both to sit down in and to rise up from. So *you* must suffer the curse of comfort. It goes with being a young guest."

And I relaxed on the cushions and the padded arm under my elbow. "And your new book . . . ?"

"—will use the same logical method. I hope it will allow me to cease to think about that book of crisis and the horrendous incidents that followed from it and which ignorant readers still want to believe somehow my book caused, rather than see it as an attempt to proffer an alternative before the world made horrifically manifest the hell my book was forged in."

"I have read that one too," I said. And, indeed, I'd entertained my own doubts as to whether it was a good book or a bad one. I had been foolish enough to bring along a copy and I put my hand on my wallet. But would it be foolish to show him that I had it? Had it been other than a barely disguised shout of ungodly obscenities as so many others had already accused it of being, or a violent hurling of fuel to burn down the world tree and the church and the castle as much as the hovel beside the plowed field, notions that would bring ruin to the village burgher as well as the country vagabond? "Your theological-political treatise."

He nodded.

"If we could look at God differently," I said, giving him the best of the most generous summaries I'd read of it, "give up our miracles, concentrate on what we do understand in the world and try to increase that understanding, rather than invest all our thinking in what we don't or can't or couldn't understand, we could also start to think about politics differently."

"You are so generous in summary," he said, smiling, "I don't know if I should even trust you."

"I was in another country," I said. "But I know *some* of what happened here. And I was here two years ago——"

"It was published a little bit before we had our *rampjaar*—not after. But the important part is that we had one."

"We heard about that even in Germany." I smiled. "It's *only* ten days away."

"That year when the people were *redeloos*, the government was *radeloos*, and the surrounding countryside was——"

"—*reddeloos*," I finished.

"You have some Dutch, then? I'd forgotten you might."

"None at all," I said. "Other than *good morning*, *good night*, and *where is the water closet*, those three are the only ones I trust myself to use." And calling a smart servant woman my age—I remembered now—old and silly.

"There are good Dutchmen today of whom you'd believe *redeloos*, *radeloos*, and *reddeloos* are the only words they need to know in the language. And I expect that will be the case for many, many years to come."

"*Redeloos, radeloos, reddeloos.*" Then I translated the words into Hebrew. "They put a very different light on *emet veshalom.*"

He repeated them in Latin. "In the *rampjaar*, the year of the disaster, the people were deranged, the government was desperate, and the countryside totally insane." He moved a slipper on the waxed and polished boards, moved his hand in the dark folds on his knee. "I think the surrounding countryside, which, bluntly, in this small nation has never been a bastion of sanity and was then, yes, under our growing hardships becoming more and more *reddeloos*—well, the countryside is where much of the tragedy, including the need for me to write my book and publish it, was forged—"

"It said it was published in Hamburg. Oldenburg said that was for your own protection." I was thinking about the homily I had read over the doorway on the Jew's house the previous morning. (Is lying for your own and others' protection an act of peacefulness—or is it just a lie?) And, yes, I was thinking of it sadly, and even accusingly—though I had agreed with almost as much of it as I had the *Principia philosophiae cartesianae*.

"I had written my *Tractatus*, published it—anonymously, yes. I wanted it to go out as pure, ungrounded idea, a message of truth with no context at all to distort it."

"The way some talk about it suggests it has already broken the pillars and brought the Temple crashing down on our heads." I paused. "I recall hearing the news, four or five years ago, while I was in Leipzig, at the University Library—two of your own supporters were torn apart in the street by the mob. That must have been hard for you."

At that moment I couldn't tell whether the man before me was here or many years away—and I wondered why, as he was only thirteen years older than I, and four years older than Gunter, right then he looked as if he were an old, old man at least a decade beyond his own years.

"There have never been many people I dined with, even intermittently, or, indeed, who received me the way I am receiving you. And six years ago, I did it no more frequently than I do now. Only with a slightly clearer head." He pulled himself up in the chair. "I heard the shouts and I went outside to see what it was. I went as quickly as I could along the streets between me and the jail. I *saw* the bloody bodies of those two men—strung by their heels like animals outside a butcher shop, naked. In bits and pieces I got a tangled story from those around me. Jan had just come back to the country. His older brother Cornelius had already been imprisoned, and Jan had only been coming to comfort the man. You understand, these are the two people in the country who were working night and day for the betterment of the people, for the government, for the nation. And yes, for the countryside. They were striving for peace with the warring French so that we would not have to waste our youth in battles we could not win—and fighting those idiots who declared war a wondrous thing that, no matter how many men it slaughtered and how many fields it trampled underfoot, made them money nevertheless, and from which they would not spare a guilder for the orphaned families whose deaths had given it to them. But those were not the men tied to the rack and slaughtered.

"There they were, one headless, one with his hands hacked off, hanging like two mutton carcasses from a gibbet on the raised octagon of stones in front of the jail. In such times, to draw any attention to yourselves at all, whether you are working for good or for ill, is to draw all the love a people can show or all the rage. And one can shift to the other like a breeze on an autumn day. They ate them, you know . . ." He nodded, as if he questioned whether I heard that.

I frowned. "Sir . . . ?"

"They cut pieces of their bodies off, and gave them to the people, who took them and . . . ate them."

Somehow in the three years since the *rampjaar* I had not learned this, No one at Gunter's had mentioned anything to me, the last time I spent a spring month in the city two years back. "Assuming you speak the truth—"

"I do."

"Why in the world would anyone—would anyone, I mean anyone in a civilized city—do that?" I could certainly see why no one in civilized circles outside the Dutch Republic had spoken of it . . . at least in the circles in which *I* moved.

His robe, I noticed, was worn. And though the floor was waxed, had the rugless room been at Gunter's house, carpenters would have refinished the boards by hand.

"Why? Because they were poor men and women in the city who had poorer sisters and cousins and parents and grandparents, and their own children out in the country—the *reddeloos* countryside; and the tales had been coming back for months about how, because there was no food and the water was polluted and the rich were burning stores rather than sharing them with their own workers, those relatives in this outlying town and that one had been reduced to eating one another—"

My face had begun to crawl over the bones of my skull, pushed by one muscle and another.

"—and those men and women rioting around the jailhouse wanted, wanted before all else, wanted before humanity, or efficiency, or justice, or compassion to do something, anything that had some legible meaning! And before any criticism had occurred, their desire had become in that day, those hours, the *only* thing meaningful." He sighed. "Why do we do anything, make any gesture, grunt or cry or scream, write our treatise on the imperceptible nightly movement of the stars or record the annual crops beside the flooding Necker or the Nile, the tides in the Thames or the movement and twists of a leaf bumping along beside a log at the edge of the Rhine or the Euphrates? Because it happened, and we were struck by it. Or we can think about its happening. And because we can say it or write it, it makes us feel as if we might have been there with someone else." He chuckled. "Only then do we sit back and figure out how, while we're at it, we might use that urge to better the world—to do something else besides maniacally and in the most brutal and inflationary way resurrect Hammurabi.

"I had written my book of crisis already—and little good it had done, not for Jan or Cornelius. Even when they break my heart, usually injustices don't incense me so. But I rushed back home—I was not sick to my stomach, I was not sick in my heart; that all came later—

"I was furious!

"I snatched out a piece of vellum and swiped up a burnt coal from the dead fire, and wrote a sign to tell the people what barbarians they were, what pigs they'd become. I was trying to take it out into the streets when the woman you met here, who brought me down, looked up from the washing, read what I'd written on it—well, she had to stop me bodily from going out! She grabbed the sign, threw it across the room, grabbed *me*. 'You will be next, you idiot!'

"'I don't care, cow!'

"'I don't *care* if you call me a cow! I'm not letting you go out there waving your intentions to commit suicide on a sign above your shoulder.' We fought in the house here while I raged that I didn't care:

"'You're trying to stop me because you want my rent! You want my body! You want the pleasure of dominating something wiser and weaker than you! You're as bad as they are! You *are* them! You are too selfish and greedy to let me do what I—'"

He sighed. "But she won.

"'No,' she said at last, breathing hard, when I was sitting on the floor and she was sitting on a table corner. 'I want to stop you because you are a good old man—as good as I too thought those poor corpses strung up outside the jail yard. No, they did not have me to their house the way they had you. But I was here sometimes when they came to see you. They came *here*.' Wasn't that a kind thing to say—even if she was lying? Does it matter whether it was her truth? Or if she wanted me to think it was because it could make me or both of us, right then and there, feel a little better? But ten minutes of the cruelties of life had turned us from two good friends to an old man with a skinned knee and twisted shoulder, and a big woman with one braid hanging down by the arm of her dress I'd torn and a bruise under her right eye that it had certainly not been my intention to give her. My outrage and arrogance had made us go at it like a pimp and a whore tussling behind the lowest tavern. Some people think philosophers can't know the passions. Ha! Might does not make right. Still, sometimes it even wins when on the side of compassion. And it gave me time to think: 'One must speak the truth.' Especially when there is nothing else one has to give. But she'd stopped me, nevertheless.

"I am alive, not dead.

"We are"—he shrugged, smiled—"still friends."

And the door opened. We both looked up. With a tray and two bowls, she stood there.

"Now, you see," he said, "I was just telling my visitor what a good woman you are, and what an even more exemplary landlord. Not every landlord will save the life of a tenant."

She said, "It's his breakfast time. I thought I'd bring in a bowl of potato and onion soup for you—with dill. That's the way *he* likes it . . ."

"Why, that's kind of you," I said.

"I'm going to be taking a bowl out to your driver—if that wouldn't be amiss with you, sir?"

"Not at all," I said. "I'm sure he will appreciate it as much as I will this one. Thank you."

So she brought the tray around, and I took a plate with the deep Dutch bowl on it, with butter and dill, and placed it beside my chair on the table where such collations had probably been set down beside family and visitors for five years, five generations? Netherlanders, like Germans, are a frugal people. (Eating one another in the country . . . ? Like a tale students might still tell in Altdorf of some woodsman's family waylaying strangers in the Black Forest during the Thirty Years' War.)

"You were angry," I said. "But you were brave. Bravery makes us like our heroes, which is important to the people who prefer liking them to despising them. Truth is what's important in the world. But is what's important always the truth?"

He sighed. "All I am saying is if the Temple comes down as easily as all that on my head or on yours, it *can't* be the true one. It's too flimsy. It falls too easily."

"Again, your understanding," I told him, "swerves dangerously close to my own." I always find myself thrown back to talk of virtue that tends to change into its opposite. Or at any rate is always putting us in a position from which that looks suspiciously to be the case.

"I suppose," he said, "it appears dangerous to some when an ordinary lens grinder in The Hague seems to think too much like a German duke and courtier, with all the advantages the Landgraves of Saxony can confer."

In last night's letter, I had mentioned Duke John Frederick.

"Lens grinders in The Hague are not whom I think of when I think of ordinary people—Van Leeuwenhoek is also in The Hague. I'm planning to see him as well, while I'm here."

"But you are seeing him as a scientist, I assume." He nodded. "I've ground lenses for him, too. I think of him as an admirable pursuer of truth."

"As there are some who say what he has discovered are not little plants and animals, but rather little microscopic demons and devils."

The Dutch Jew (who will always remain a Jew to the rest of us, if not to himself, even when we forget or he does; and who will remain so as long as we can say *gentile*) slid his robe over his knee. "Did Oldenburg tell you I am at the end of my work on another treatise—or nearing it? One never finishes. I'd sent him some pages of one of the earlier sections I *feel* is finished." He smiled. "At least till I want to revise it."

"He is your friend," I told him. "Not your enemy. He told me the title and the topic. Nothing more. And even if he had, I would not have bandied it about to get to the ears of your enemies who would immediately begin to drown it in premature misunderstandings."

His black hair touched only at temples and neck with gray, this Jew without a beard gave me a questioning look.

I sighed seriously. "He said it was about God. He said you've called it *Ethica*. And I must say, given your last book, as titles go that seems a radical one, if not openly dangerous: we come to it prepared to learn about God and are handed a title that suggests it's about the way men treat men."

"More than half will be just that—at least by implication."

"There are some who say that you are laughing at us. And the more serious, the more measured, the less passionate your tone, the more clearly they hear your laughter and the more painful to them is your derision."

His face grew serious. "I hope it is more radical than that—and that it's not too much more dangerous. When, in its later parts, it speaks about how men behave, it speaks about how they delude themselves into thinking they are doing things beneficial or harmless when they are not—"

"And if," I said, "that self-delusion takes place without the help of any demons or devils . . . ?"

He nodded. "It's all a set of rational errors. It suggests that rationality can fix them."

"You, sir," I said, "are a dangerous man. That's a dangerous idea and a great responsibility."

"So they are always telling me." He gave the most modest of shrugs. "Thank you, I suppose."

It's always surprised me how quickly we find ourselves considering social distinctions, especially in philosophy. I mean, if you'd spent as much of the last month reading and rereading Plato, Heraclitus, and Descartes as I have since I began this leg of what has sometimes seemed endless traveling with endless obligations, you too would sometimes find it hard to hold your thoughts in check: Plato and Heraclitus were, after all, princes. And Descartes worked (as do I) for princes. For small talk I went back to something less accusatory:

"Truly to get away from the notion of philosophy as a princely calling you have to go—not to Socrates (he worked for Plato, after all, or perhaps Plato worked for him; on that metaphorical level sometimes it's hard to tell) but all the way to Diogenes of Synope, the old slave with his master too lax to keep him in check: the vagabond sleeping with the street dogs in a broken bathtub at the edge of the old slave market (because they wouldn't let him in the Agora where Plato walked and taught through some of the same years, though, with their different markets, they were really 'sparring' friends, if you read the testaments). Diogenes—pleasuring himself without shame where passersby could watch, while he, not even in rags, but unconcerned and presumably grinning, shouted his barbs about old Plato: 'Plato winces when I track dust across his rugs; he knows that I am walking on his vanity! . . . If only I could free myself from hunger as easily as from desire! . . . I've seen Plato's cups and tables, but not his cupness and his tableness!' To yell about freedom from desire with your cock in your fist, is that enough to start a revolution? Perhaps not. But he's always been a character in every account I've known."

"Plato's fool, some think—without whom Plato cannot truly be understood." He nodded.

We talked on. I spoke more with him in Hebrew, because I prided myself on my conversational command of all the classical languages. I'd heard enough gentiles speak Hebrew with Jews to know that was no guarantee they'd get on, any more than if both spoke Estonian or Norwegian to one another. But we did. Why? Some of it I can guess at. (She owned the building, it seemed. Herr Spinoza was her—and her husband's, who was not there that day—favorite and, now, only tenant. Had been for years. What was theirs was his. And I was ready to admit the mug of Dutch beer she eventually brought was really more flavorful than the German brew Gunter had laid in for my visit to the great Venice of the North.) Still other elements were as indecipherable as the fact that he was green eyed and I was missing a right rear molar that had shattered when, as a child, I'd bitten down on a clamshell for the fun of it—the kind of fact that makes you wonder from time to time: Does that have anything to do with his or my becoming a philosopher?

Of the diplomatic visits I expected to carry out for my lord-ship during my visit to Amsterdam, this is the one that I'd wanted to make the most—the one that was entirely for me. I had set it up by and for myself. I remember sitting, thinking, while he was going on and momentarily my mind drifted:

Sixteen, seventeen *is* old to learn Latin. Or Greek.

My new acquaintance, Spinoza, was the opposite of the sort of prodigy I had aspired to be since my childhood; I started tu-toring in all three languages probably younger than this one had started his Hebrew alone.

But allow me once more to appeal to Diogenes who said Plato's philosophy was an endless conversation. I think the truth he points to there is something that pretty much any bright youngster who actually reads the greatest of our philosophers can quickly intuit. Yes, it's an endless conversation, and what's more, it's an endless conversation in which the parts of the various

participants can only be played by aspects of a single conscious-
ness. Plato's discussants and querents are not polite as students
and teachers are polite. They are polite the way only fantasy discussants can be civil inside a fantasy. Were they real, they'd be at
each other's throats before eight or nine pages were done.

But we talked—in Hebrew. Then Latin. And now and again
our language so enfolded us that our minds appeared to do the
same. I had felt as much when I'd read his *Tractatus*. And there
is nothing to make someone feel that a writer or a thinker is
important like the belief—not now and again, but again and
again—that his argument is right first; and only more or less
clearly put, second; or believable, third.

We talked. Together.

And somehow all dialectical incongruences were filled in by
the language that seemed proper—by words, gestures, facial ex-
pressions, which is to say: yes, here and there, on a surprisingly
deep level, we found ourselves agreeing.

I've talked to him. I've read what he's written. Certainly he
seems as skeptical of miracles as I am: this alone prompts me to
read and even reread his argument, even if different from mine.
And I do think, at this point, now that I have, we are equally
rigorous against the miraculous.

How many specificities I recall about that room on that
morning, details that will last the length of time this journal
entry endures and that will vanish as soon the last copy crumbles
or the last citizen forgets the language, details that might compel
many to decide that either there is or there isn't (it doesn't matter) a specific order of roomness for that room, or two specific
orders of roomness for that room (modest, not in the best repair,

unassuming) as opposed to this room (generally more likely to last but with secret flaws entailed in the kinds of people who come to confer in it, spend a few days in it, grow up in it; as well as true architectural instabilities that will not give way till long after the other building is pulled down, and some inner mystery—or external plot—causes this one to go up in flames or crumble into the crevice of an earthquake the size of Lisbon's, or to fall to a marauding army)—as I said before, we talked.

And in that talk, he chose to tell me this tale, as if it followed from what he'd been saying. I hadn't been listening all that carefully, but because it did follow so clearly from what I'd been thinking, I knew I must have understood him anyway.

"You know, sir, when I was a boy, and still lived in the city, I remember it was an early spring, but which spring I'm rather unsure at this point. But with my father I'd gone to visit the house of a merchant friend. I was in the back, waiting for my father to come out. Over his front door were carved the Hebrew words that dramatize so much of the best in mankind—"

I recited in Hebrew, "'Truth and peace form the foundation of the world . . .'"

"You've seen it?"

"Yesterday morning, I saw it over the door of a merchant in the city."

"Several houses have taken it for their motto. But not mine." He smiled, nodded. "I was sitting in the back, in their garden—in summer—waiting for my father to finish, when I looked down at a table beside me, I saw a leaf—it was an all but windless day, not like today with its early winter airs—and I began to think, the way we do at that age: 'Why can't I move that leaf with my mind—the way the mind of God is supposed to move the world?' So I looked at the leaf, there on the planks, and narrowed my eyes. And I thought as intensely as I could without making a sound: Leaf, move! And it didn't. It just lay there. So once again, I thought: *Leaf, move!* And still it was still. So for a third time I gathered all my inner strength and prepared myself once more and—" He let out a breath. "But suddenly I knew, I saw, I *experienced* why I could not move the leaf with my thoughts. It was because the leaf on the table and my thought, I now knew, I now sensed, were two separate orders of ontological existence. The leaf was material and so was the wind that moved it. But thoughts were of the same ontological order as images, artworks, ideas. My thought could not move the leaf for the same reason that if I pulled a print of a winter storm from the pile of prints the merchant kept among his stores, and brought it into the garden, and set it up on the table so that its images of storm and rough weather faced the tree directly, not a leaf or a branch nor a gnat or wisp of dust would move because of that storm. That's because thoughts modeled by material and material that provokes thoughts *don't* interact. They could no more affect one another directly, without the mode of a body between, than could a drawing of a cannon just having fired fell a real and clopping cavalryman. The mind of God can't be exempt from such restrictions, because it obtains to what mind, thoughts, and material are. Three minutes later, with hardly a move, I had figured out why there could be no miracles. Miracles entail the thoughts of God directly and without material intervention controlling matter itself. God's thoughts couldn't control the world—not because *my* mind or *my* thoughts weren't strong enough, but rather because that's not how thoughts work in the world. Any thoughts. If they could, they'd belong to another ontological order and, by definition, would be something other than thoughts. They'd have to be something that *could* interact with material directly, and the only thing we know of that can do that *is* other material. If God wants to move materials in an unusual way, He will have to set up still other material situations and events—possibly visible, possible hidden—to bring it about. But that's why there aren't any miracles, because thought and material work the way they do." He shrugged. "It's all over the book I've already been so rash as to publish—though I haven't come out and said it in so many words. I am working on the other now, where I'm planning on putting it clearly and succinctly among the first set of definitions on which all else will depend, possibly even as the very first definition. Or the second . . ."

Finally I said I must go. He said he would like to see me again. Surprising myself, I asked him what about tomorrow. Surprising me equally, he said that he would be delighted. He had little to do but grind lenses—and think.

At any rate because I had been thinking along the preparatory lines for this argument just as he had, I had no trouble understanding it.

He concluded: "And it felt very good to have such thoughts in a garden behind a house bearing that legend on its door, but that was just an extra, a little stutter to the event, the reward of pleasure added to the event, given us by God or nature."

And this lack of confusion, right then and there, seemed the most natural thing in God's world, enough to make me think, in this most particular of possible worlds, that it might be taken for a truth rather than a miracle that nature and God might be not only one, but be the *kind* of one, the order of one, that he thought they were.

He repeated, ". . . *Deus sive Natura*." He had said it once before, but now I could understand what it meant: *God or in other words nature* . . . "I am really looking forward to continuing our conversation tomorrow, even if we go on from what we talked about today, or simply go back over what we've already talked about, perhaps deepening our understanding of it, enriching it with more examples, more details."

Was it a different Jew? Was it the same? Was it unimportant . . . ?

"I expect," he said, "there will be some of both—going on and going over. I am sure you have learned by now that that is the only way any real learning worth the word can proceed." We stood, ready to leave each other now that we had set a time for the two of us to meet again. I felt his book in the pocket of my greatcoat—and at the same time, he sighed and said, "I wish my eyes were good enough for me to read my old texts—just to enjoy the clarity of my own thinking. I mean other than when I sit down for a real work session, with a lens for reading, a lens for writing, the sunlight or a lamp. I am not a practical inventor, as I have heard rumors that you are. Rumors of your calculating machines have preceded you."

I thought of the one in my trunk I'd been planning to give Gunter. "When I come tomorrow, I can bring one to show you. They are cunning. I've given away a few to really important men of the world. But they're very costly to have made, so that one—"

"—hesitates to give one to a half-blind old man of forty, who will clearly not be able to return the favor with anything of equal worth?"

I did not frown. But I was thrown back to the not very propitious start to our still—in my mind—pleasant encounter, and wondered if the beginning (and the end) were doomed not to be its strong points. (There are reasons civilized people don't talk of money. But, of course, I was the one who'd brought it up.)

"Please," he said. "You mustn't worry. Keep it. I'm sure others would appreciate it more. And I'm not wanting for one, sir."

"Philosophers have been famous," I said, "for saying the obvious and giving us a laugh by it—Diogenes—or getting killed for it, as when Archimedes told the soldier to stand away from his sunlight."

We both laughed.

And the landlord knocked, entered, and, shrugging up her shawl, told us that my carriage was ready. My driver had awakened. She had brought him a roll and a bowl. He was now finished. "And our friend here, once noon's past, does get tired . . ."

"Of course," I said. And rose.

"You mustn't worry about me," he said. "If they try to arrest me for atheism because God, if it's anything, must be a being separate from the world who controls it from without, rather than a system of forces controlling it from within, I will simply have our friend here tell them I am hiding in the attic, when in fact I have gone out into the world to walk among the winter drifts by the canals, among the summer leaves of the garden that sigh and sag under the rains." At least—I will admit it to this journal—that's the best job I could do reconstructing it.

For a moment I thought of the lace makers in the dim polishing room at Gunter's, weaving thread and fabric as though thread were language and they were poets. I'd quipped then that they'd seemed to be weaving for their lives. Now, from what I'd learned of the *rampjaar*, I wondered if perhaps they were—as, indeed, I now knew this Jew was no poet of Latin, but spoke from as great a sense of crisis as any poet could.

At one point I'd told him a proof I'd worked out for the existence of God.

"That's actually rather clever." He looked quite pleased. "Do you think you could jot that down for me?"

"It's not *that* clever," I told him. "I wouldn't stand by it today. I thought enough of it when I first did it, however."

"Still, I'd like to think about it a bit and make sure arguments of that structure are addressed, at least indirectly, in the work I'm just finishing up."

"Certainly," I said. And did—twice. And took one with me so I'd remember its details as well.

Possibly because of that, I include one more tale he told. I put it here, paradoxically enough, at the end of the things I remember in order, though it was not the last thing he told me. The fact is, I can't remember on which side of his revelation in the garden it fell. (Doesn't every philosopher these days have one?) The man I hope to encounter in London had his in a garden, too, where an apple fell at his feet—or hit him on the head. He's been telling that story to one Royal Society member or another since '66. Wish he'd pin it down on paper so we'd all know what he's talking about or if it makes sense! But in this journal, putting it at the end of the account of what I remember Spinoza telling me is a way, specifically, of marking that it is not the end, it is not the conclusion, it was not the moment I have understood most exactly or the best summary of what's gone before, either of context or content. Rather, it's the one most open to revision, rethinking, correction.

So at one point, he mentioned: "Because I started learning the languages in which basically I've lived—Latin and, soon, Greek—so late, I was particularly aware of the gifts they immediately began to give me, whereas someone who picks up an ancient language as a child of four or five is first aware of them the way one is aware of old, comfortable toys with their painted faces half worn away. Reassuring—but not exciting." (Had he written this once in a journal to himself?) "Despite the fact that words, images, ideas, *Vorstellen* all share an ontology that is easiest to talk about metaphorically as images and art, one understand this most clearly when one explains language's specific relation to a specific body, because a body is the material interface of matter and mind. I was led by those historical paths that Latin and Greek create for us among the living European languages my father and his business acquaintances had to speak for work to *use* philosophers from the past, not just Ignatius and Clement of Alexandria, not only the church fathers forbidden me by my own people, not just the endless conversation of Plato or the fragments of Heraclitus, the stories of Thales and Anaximenes, the fragment of Anaximander, Parmenides, the poets such as Xenophanes who could have been philosophers or theologians as well, or even Plato's Diotima, who believed love could heal real wounds dealt by the sword of God himself, or Hypatia of Alexandria, who believed both in mathematics and magic. Whose brilliance was it, hers or Plato's, to realize desire is the need to close a difference *Deus sive Natura* has struck into fundamental formations of the world as it has seemed to have so generously provided the many occasions for all these teachers' different lessons?"

It was the last line that brought me most sharply back (from my own thoughts, whatever they were) because that's when I realized that, like Plato, whose *Republic* upheld the education of women and their entrance into politics, our radical philosopher despite all appearances had not abandoned everything female. And could admit to having learned something, as it occurs to me now, from wrestling bodily with a woman.

But as well as admitting all this questioning and revision into the terminal place in my narrative, the place that in most discourses is reserved for terminal certainty, I have found that writing it down has made me remember something that I'd already written in an only partially remembered state. I've written it. If you've read this whole section, you've read it too.

(Who am I talking to other than myself here? Someone I hope who at least knows my languages.) But what I've already written several hours ago now and you've read whenever was actually what I felt he'd probably said (as much of it as I could remember), enhanced by what I thought he must have meant, as best I could make it out. But only minutes back, in a pause between sentences, it returned to me, with clarity and certainty.

This is what now came back to me verbatim:

> Trying to arrest me for atheism, given the specificity of
> my arguments, is like hunting for a man hiding in the

attic of a building that has none, when in truth he is sitting in the back garden of another house, working diligently on his own concerns, in another neighborhood entirely.

Does this mean that his atheist in the attic was finally different from mine? Or perhaps that mine can talk to his from now on? And since we are letting this rethinking move us more firmly back to truth, the thought about the lacemakers was, actually, not one I'd had in The Hague but rather one I'd had here when I was misremembering what he'd said and what I'd thought it might have been. A real thought of my own, but—I confess—my placement of it was a lie—a lie with which it is easier to dispense, having now arrived at the same truth.

7.

How does it happen? Either the peasants or the powerful stamp their feet (or eat their enemies) on the continent which goes out not as a message written on a parchment and tied to a pigeon's foot sent through the air and collected at the other end, but more like ripples sent across the surface of ink from a drop fallen into an inkwell, and it passes across the waters to England, which responds with troops and a tirade that strikes fear not only in the men and women of the Netherlands but in all the nations around.

Is the ink itself, the sea itself, the Great Mind of God that carries the message? If not, then the message moves through the minds of men with all its terrors, with all its horrors, and I don't know if we can bear that. Our radical Jew tells us it is carried not by the mind of anything but rather by the structure of nature to which all individual minds are merely a variety of over-interested responses, which is even more frightening, because we are the ink in which are written other messages that we cannot even understand.

Is that my madness?

Or his?

Or is it a *folie à deux*, from two men neither of whom has been prepared by education or experience in the world, or in the world's extant mechanics, to understand it or each other fully?

Just after some church had rung its bells on the second hour after noon, I left by the front steps to see if my carriage was still parked outside. Twelve feet along the block, where we'd pulled up before sunrise, the heavy driver again lay on the bench under his lumpy blanket.

I looked up to see that below a November gray like carded dust the house was red brick and three stories, with a stone cornice, no attic, and a level roof. Why did I bring my eyes down? On the second floor I caught a shutter closing.

From street level, I heard the catch.

Climbing into the carriage, I noticed the leather hinges were quite as loose as they'd been on the drive out before sunup. I was about to call to my driver to start, but the vehicle's sag at my ascent must have wakened him. I heard him grunt, then felt the first shifting in the carriage as he rose upright. One of the horses stepped around—its shoes clinked the cobbles. We pulled a few inches forward, then drifted back; I settled onto the seat and shoved my own winter blanket to the padded wall.

The driver shook the reins to still them. "Sir . . . ?" he asked from above.

"Yes," I said, "ready," and hoped he'd found some side street in which to relieve himself during the hours I'd been inside.

Wisely, I'd asked to use the water closet in the back of the house, with its ceramic amphora and the little long-handled pan for splashing down the planks if anything got stuck: good working-class manners said you cleaned it yourself, while good manners at Gunter's said you left it for the gardeners to do each dawn and evening. Only the poorest folk—often lame or one-eyed or deaf, or with a withered arm (broken and not properly set)—were such assistants at Gunter's; they never came inside the house. I still recall Gunter explaining proudly, two years ago, that he was going to have a slanted wall built down the inside of his latrine, so his doctor (or he himself . . . ?) could examine his stool if necessary.

Examinations of fecal leavings tell much about a man's or a woman's health.

The first time this morning I'd used the place, I'd noticed the building he'd planned hadn't been done yet—or had been done and undone. (I wondered if some story lay behind it, or was it only a good—or not so good—idea no one had ever got round to.) Sitting in the carriage as we rumbled and joggled behind the horses, I wondered why I'd let my fancies roam so far afield.

Me, I'd left nothing to be splashed on the inside walls of Spinoza's four-square Dutch water closet. (I looked.) And I couldn't even remember—or was it just that I didn't want to— whether I had on Gunter's, since my arrival in Amsterdam the day before. Would such universal necessities ever be brought indoors, I wondered? And to whose maintenance would they then be assigned, and would it be different from now . . . ?

8.

As I rode back home, that red-brick Hague house drifted behind and a foggy November city afternoon became a country November night with a moon and discarded clouds aslant the horizon as we returned to the Venice of the North, the city of water and donkeys and cheese. For a while I thought: Sometime we fear the Jews' control of our lives, the way we fear so often that servants can run—and run away with—a great house wherever the least laxness is allowed. Diogenes, who was a homeless slave two and a half millennia ago, used to declare that it was not such a bad thing, but one that wise men should wish for, if their slaves—he was a slave and said *slaves*—were smart enough to make the system work to everyone's profit.

There's a form that waits for a fiction, a story old as any everyday tale: one, two, three . . . Choose an event. (That's one.) Begin with what happened before it and tell it, concentrating on what caused it. (That's two.) Once you've moved on to tell the tale itself, tell what its outcome was—and it's over. (That's three and done.) You'd think you could squeeze such accounts comfortably into three days. But the fact is, real events seldom leave such simple narrative forms intact, any more than the shit on the boards of the water shaft tells all . . . True stories want to go on for years. They want to wriggle back to beginnings before the flood. Or they want to stop as abruptly as—

Well, as that dash there.

We Europeans have a set of systems in which for centuries, outside Russia, Jews were not allowed to own land and so were forced to work in cities. They suffered severe restrictions on the ways in which they were allowed to survive. Having confined them to trade, we seemed surprised when we blinked and found them dominating it! In fifteenth-century Italy, we made them wear black and yellow handkerchiefs and their citizenry put on races along the Corso for the pleasure of the aristocracy.

And every forty or fifty years, soldiers were dispersed to slaughter the inhabitants of one or another of their villages. After centuries of such oppressions, it's rather arrogant to claim surprise at any possible retaliation, whether aimed at the perpetrators or passed on to a whole new set of victims, reread conveniently as more oppressors. Even so, around and between our atrocities, they develop a life, a culture, a way to negotiate the world we shaped for them, so that soon they seem to be as invaluable . . . well, as servants in a capably run home.

But when the most frightening Jew of all appears—or has already appeared and been writing, thinking, forming his . . . but what is he forming? We know only it has been going on a decade or more. Or, who knows, going on even longer and blossoming when it does because of the extraordinary pressures upon it. What is the first we hear of him?

His own community cannot tolerate his deviations from the strict reactionary structures they've evolved to make themselves invaluable to their own oppressors any more than the oppressors themselves can, nor does *he* have any serious desire to side with we who oppress. He simply wants to sit and think, to walk about and think, to look at things already arrayed about him and observe what there is about them that has not necessarily been thought before.

If such a man, with such a history, found such a world intolerably evil and worthy of immediate devastation by an angry, resentful God, how could anyone be surprised?

The amount of agony and suffering that must have been deployed to bring it to its present form!

How could any of us, gentile or Jew, be surprised—wouldn't we rather breathe a sigh of logical relief?

But that he should look at it with a calm eye, should find things in it that are beautiful, that he should hesitate to look beneath the surface at the evil that supports all things and instead see the beauty of surfaces and think how they may be logically linked without causing any more pain, rather than trying to pay back every little bit of pain caused in the past, as if forgetting and dying were even more humane for the group than forgiving and praying were for the individual . . .

How terrible that, with a serious knowledge of what had been done, he could find the world beautiful because beauty was a potential to be gambled on as much as an accomplishment to be coveted, that at best the world was intriguingly devious and only the people in it a little silly.

That the world I live in could produce such a man is—frankly—as humbling as the fact that it could produce more than one of him, that it could produce so many so like each other, among all our differences.

Which includes me, arriving with a pile of spoiled small-clothes and a smile for a grubby young Dutchman who, at least for now, finds it both fascinating as well as a fine diversion in his day's drudgeries to wash them, for which I will give him an extra coin.

That this Jew and I would come so close to the same conclusions, as different as we are, I find even more humbling. For I've always felt that this is a very good world, the best world that, given what we have to work with, it could be—and that's even with the silliness.

9.

That night, instead of going right to bed after my grim, chill supper of fish and bread, I was joined by Gunter for a glass in the dining room. We lit no candelabra. He struck up a single lamp, placed it on a copper charger, and transferred it from the linen mantel cloth to the lace tablecloth.

On some napkins whipped out from a drawer in the sideboard, he set two glasses and poured from a ceramic bottle.

I was already sitting on my side of the table. He came back, set down the glasses. Mine had the color of pale straw. I looked up.

He said, "Genever."

I assumed his the same.

Then he went around to his side of the table and lowered himself to his chair with its scrolled arms. "Gottfried, I don't know how you do it. You seem to keep it all in order. I can't. I really can't. You'd think my brain was going. My parents were so much better at this than I am. At least, with all their craziness, they seemed to be. Sometimes I just want to go off to the country—to *another* country—and live in a cave. Take one of the menservants with me. Peytor? At least I can bear his personality. Though he only knows two languages—one is Walloon or something: nothing that could do anyone in any part of the civilized world any good."

"If he's a nice boy," I said, "probably you could teach him to be a body servant in a few weeks, a few months." For all I didn't know about him, it's surprising how complete a picture of him I put together.

Gunter frowned at me, his glass gleaming between his fingers, his brow bedeviled by the light's low source. "Are you serious?"

I shrugged. "As serious as you." I sipped. (How various people in various parts of the world drink the various things they do has always been a fascinating thing to contemplate. A bit of ananas, a bit of juniper, a bit of malt . . . ? All those tiny tastes in one glass. Gunter is a good sort, a loyal friend. But drinking it, I was reminded of how he used to love practical jokes back in Altfort. Now I think about some of his current attempts to oblige that are almost as annoying.)

"Have you ever *talked* to that boy? He's a charmer—in the way so many country folk are when they get to the city and learn they have nothing to sell *but* their charm. Over the years, I *have* talked to him, for an hour there, another hour here. Yes, he's clever, funny, sometimes a delight. But he's also . . . *very* stupid. Mary already knows what a body servant is about, for a woman or for a man. If I took her off to a cave, I'm sure she'd be as efficient there as she is here. And I'd die of boredom if she was the only other person there." He took another sip. "Peytor *can't* learn. His head is so filled with fancies and foolishness, there's no room for information. I know it. She knows it. I can stand him as her assistant. She likes him too, as does everyone, and she feels sorry for him and cuts him an unlimited number of second chances. I say he's her assistant. He's more her pet—as, frankly, he's become mine. And, if you actually lived here for any length of time, probably he'd become yours unless your heart is far colder than I assume it to be. Preoccupied? Yes. Hard-hearted? That's not you, Gottfried. But that's why she consents to work with him and keep him out of trouble. You don't have to know that about Peytor. You're only here for a couple of weeks, every two years or so. You can smile at the advancement he makes, and don't have to worry over the advancements he doesn't." He chuckled. "He's just right where he is, thanks to Mary and Otto, and Otto—that's old Otto with the beard, who sleeps in the barn in the back—but thanks to all of them really, both the ones who mostly like him and those who constantly lose patience. We form just the proper emulsion that, when someone like yourself arrives, keeps his better points polished and tends to submerge from sight his bad ones—of which there are a considerable number. Though he's not a thief or a backbiter, or a practitioner of evils and pernicious magics, now and again he gets accused of all of them. And against all of them, as against the sophistication of the city, his stupidity is his best defense."

10.

Though I was born in Saxony's capitol, Leipzig, that city is in the rural stretches of my country, so it was in some of the smaller outlying towns that I learned that the great houses often did their laundry over a week or so, twice per year—or some of them in a single year would do it only once. Everyone who has any contact with such a home learns that you do not arrive, unannounced, during laundry week. But the simple propinquity of resources and labor in cities makes it likely that wealthy families who choose to live in Leipzig, not to mention Venice or Amsterdam, find such infrequency impractical and are impelled to wash clothes every six weeks. It turns on how many services as well as how many repairmen and workers are available. It has to do with how many servants live in the house and how many live off grounds as well as how many family members live together, and whether all of them can afford to keep seventy shirts just for daily wear and what appearances are desired and what such standards require in maintenance. In both the town and the country, the poor are notorious for rarely washing when work is oppressive. They want to imitate those better off than they are, so when they can afford to wash, they do. But with the illness and oppression they suffer, all too many of the poor, young and old, not only cease to wash but often go naked—or close enough to it. And sometimes, so do the rich.

"I put a few grains of the baron's salts in my glass. He says they bring a man relaxing sleep. Really, he's an amazing doctor, one step away from a wizard. Do you want to try some?"

"Oh. Why, no. I'll forgo that." So Gunter's night drink was not the same as mine. But I sleep quite well enough without taking up a new habit, a new addiction.

Is a poet someone who only wants to describe things, while a philosopher is someone who wants to describe things so that they will reflect and even explain the differences and forces that relate them all and hold them all together?

Or sometimes tear them apart.

Is the rarity of washing a hardship because of need or because of habit? And to whom is it a hardship? Or is it an easing of responsibility? And what does it mean—in the city, in the country—when, naked or clothed, I turn on you, tear you apart, and eat you?

What does it mean about habits?

Mean to the philosopher?

To the poet?

And what does it mean to want to understand this, rather than—or at least before—you condemn it or forgive it?

11.

After my first day with Senhor de Spinoza (his family, I know, were merchants from Portugal), I was wondering what he might do with such a toy as I had brought with me. Or, really, would it pave relations more smoothly if I took it on to England and dropped it off at the Royal Society with a note to pass it on to the Great Man himself at Trinity (or, indeed, vice versa)? Still, I was curious what Spinoza might make of the design of my toy, as much as I was curious about Newton or the rumors—

There was a knock.

"Yes . . . ?"

It was young, fresh-looking, extremely Dutch Peytor. I realized he looked rather better than, of a sudden, I now *remembered* him from two years ago! (As soon as I'd seen him, I *did* remember him!) For one thing he wore shoes—wooden ones. And he was of an age at which he might have even gained a final spurt of growth while I'd been away. "Good day." I smiled. "Seeing you now makes me realize why I didn't recognize you this morning when you were unloading the carriage. They haven't graduated you to the house, now—have they?"

"They let me in," he said. Blue eyes, a wide mouth, yellow hair that was actually a *little* darker than in memory. "The last time you were here, I would mostly sneak in." He looked at me expectantly—and I began to frown because, at that point, I really didn't know what he was expecting.

"Yes, boy . . . ?"

"Herr Leibniz, I thought . . . well, I thought you might have something for me . . . to do."

"What do you mean?"

"Laundry—your personal laundry. Like the last time."

"Oh, God in his heaven," I said. "You remembered *that*?" But now I was surprised I didn't. "Usually I hope that someone who encounters my eccentricity in that area will forget it or be good enough to pretend to. No, young man, I don't. I've only been here a day."

"Last time"—he looked like a hungry sheep (not sheepish; like a sheep looking around for grass)—"when you snared me out in the garden with the promise of a coin, you brought me to the back door, went up to your room, and came down again with *three* sets for me."

"That, truly, I don't remember. But I go through smallclothes so frequently in this house or that house, I lose track."

"Well, I remember it was June. Now it's November." (I beckoned him in.) "It's hotter in June." He did not come in, but stood there uncomfortably. "When it's hot and one perspires a great deal, you said, you go through three sets in a day. But at this time of year, you can get by with one—or, sometimes you use two if you have a formal dinner. You said that to me."

He had a good memory. "I'm eccentric, yes, but I'm not insane. Probably I said you *could* go through three in a day. But I don't think I often do. And at this time of year, you can get by with one." Though it's true: long years back I'd decided never to have children, since if I passed on my genius, I would certainly have passed on my eccentricity, as I often feared they were the same thing in different contexts. The genius is what people celebrated. The pain is what genius knows alone. "Peytor, come back in a couple of days. The weather has spared you a job. Also, if I remember right, last time I had come from Germany, rather than France, where the servants are much less obliging than you good fellows are here. So wait till I've collected a few more." And, you know, I actually expected he might have wanted something else.

"Oh," he said, awed. "Certainly. In a few . . . days?"

And in a moment of over-friendliness that has gotten me in trouble more than once, I remembered: "Gunter says he's sending you to spend spring with your family."

Peytor dropped his eyes. "That's what he wants me to tell people." (Indiscretion meets indiscretion.) "But I'm going to the baron's laboratory, out past Utrecht. He's going to break my leg again to see if he can fix it. I have to spend three months in his smelly cellar, healing. I'm terrified I might not come back. A man died the first time I was there. And his sister is no longer there to help take care of us. I pray for a miracle. Sometimes I want just to run away—and I would, I think, if I had any family to go to. But I don't. The country frightens me."

"Oh . . ." And with that revelation, the young man had acquired new reasons in my mind for wanting to eat his masters!

"You may go now."

With a bow he backed from the doorway—and I saw his
limp, which I had *not* remembered. (And no one had bothered
to tell me.) He closed the door, as a good servant does. The
limp made me uncomfortable. (I know how the physically
deformed of the servant class can be treated in the German
countryside—not to mention in the central cities of the
continent.)

For a moment as I stood there, I wondered if his interest
in me was, as we say, physical. (I chuckled.) Or, indeed, was in
my smallclothes. (I laughed.) Either case could be taken care
of simply enough. If he were interested in my eccentric underthings, he could take them, do what he wanted with them,
wash them, return them . . . As long as I noticed no difference
in them, why should it bother me? Servants have being doing
that with their masters' apparel as long as masters have been doing it with servants'. Smallclothes—men's or women's—are the
kind of thing that, when it changes, quite quickly gains sexual
interest, like boots shined with blood-colored polish, or the
undercoverings that make feet comfortable in boots, whether
clean or clotted with the wearer's own dirt: in my castle community some one or five of the lords or of the peasantry is likely
to like them a little too much. I've known poor men who slept
with a handkerchief with which the grand lady of the house
wiped away her pee, having fished it from the latrine, and a
prince who cherished a handful of leaves that a beggar woman
threw in the woods as he spied on her, once she swabbed away

her own. Those are the forces that hold communities together, as the sniffings and pokings and pawings of puppies keep them from wandering off from their play packs beside the pond to fall into the clutches of cougar, coyote, or some wild man with a rock who thinks roast (or raw) puppy might be succulent. How could it be otherwise with creatures like us? Indeed, I can imagine someone making just that the topic of a grand volume, a grand series of volumes, had they the leisure and time, encyclopedias and pseudoxias.

And if Peytor thought greater intercourse with me or someone of my class would further his position in life—well, that would be even simpler. Servants and their masters—men and women—have thought so since the time of Francesco Cenci (if not since Hephaestion joined Alexander's march to conquer the world, or since Theodora danced for Justinian in the markets of Byzantium and took her first step toward the throne of the Eastern Roman Empire). Said the judge when he pronounced Cenci's conviction for sodomy, "His crime is that he is a grown man doing with other grown men"—the grooms in his stable, mostly hired for the purpose—"what is only acceptable to do with boys," thus defining a moral structure that controlled both the church and the castle seventy-seven years ago in Rome as much as it controlled the world of Philip of Macedon and his son. And boys—and men—inclined to exploit or violate that structure have been snickering over it and repeating it just as long, back through Francesco's orgies with his horses, his grooms, his three wives, his sons and his daughter, through the Borgia Popes to Aristotle and Plato both.

Wait, a knock—

12.

I thought it might be a different servant, assigned to check how the first had done in preparing the room for my retiring, for my bed was already turned back when I'd come in. Mary, perhaps? But it was overeager Peytor again (who has once more, just now, half an hour past, departed), for his second visit of the evening. He wanted to know, for sure, when I would have any small-clothes ready for him to wash, and, though he hoped I wouldn't take this as forward of him, had worked himself up to come back and ask. His double thinking and rethinking seemed to have made him just as nervous as it could make me.

(*Was* this about something else? But I've encountered enough of that both in high halls and low to make me sure, if only from writing it out, that it wasn't.)

Oh, I could talk with the young follow a *few* moments at the door, as long as he was going to do something so personal as wash my soiled smallclothes.

And like a youngster too forward at an elder's smile, he stepped inside—hesitantly. Yes, he limped.

I wondered if he had been born with it—or acquired it. "Did you start working here as a gardener?"

"Yes. As an assistant—with Old Otto, outside. But now I'm in the house, with Mary." For a moment I could have sworn he was threatening me: he was someone from outside who *could* get in, despite his origin, despite his limp! (Where was Old Otto from . . . ?)

"I see," I said, and made sure that my smile held neither mocking nor condescension. (Did it hold fear . . . ?)

From garden to house, since I'd been here last, even though I didn't remember him . . . ? Was he ambitious? Or lucky? Or wiser than Gunter had assumed? Or more perverted than I had?

I tried to feel honestly pleased at his progress since my last visit, but I felt I shouldn't inquire more into it, should accept and enjoy it as he did. I asked him to come in and sit. He did, and sat carefully on the other side of the writing table from me, its ivory inlay between us, with a rough-edged sheet of blotting paper spread over it. He sat very straight. And I could not make out whether he favored the leg by sticking it out or tried to make it look normal by keeping it back against the rungs. The table between us was in the way.

We talked of duck eggs gathered from dry nests on the banks and fishermen's eel baskets along the canals. And, yes, Gunter was right—Peytor was clever but not smart. He could tell his stories, though there wasn't much to them. Still, I am as interested in servants as I am in the society they serve. But I realized I resented his withholding a means of possible interpretation from me, though it was only the writing table that blocked me. I couldn't very well ask him to move and let me see his deformity more closely. Though he was a servant, and a servant eager to please . . .

And, yes, he *was* from the countryside—

And had he lost family and friends in '73? (I felt uncomfortable asking about it because I expected the answer . . .)

Waiting for my tongue to form the next question, as he was nearing the end of his response (yes, he had; and I was too concerned with my own fears to see if he seemed sad or angry; though either could be falsely assumed), I was about to ask him if any of his family or friends had been eaten—and found myself appalled at my own forwardness. To ask that of someone from or related to the *reddeloos* countryside was *radeloos*!

And while I deflected us from such topics to less catastrophic ones about the house and the city, my heart banged under my ribs with something like fear. Though why should I fear offending such a good-natured youth? Unless he wasn't so good-natured. Was he twenty yet? I wasn't sure. And . . . *why* was I afraid? And why even more afraid that he might know my fear . . . ?

By now I wanted to know how much of his urge to get to washing my smallclothes was curiosity and how much might lie at the limen of appetite. A worldly man, as I say, I have known such things in both the young and the old, the base and the noble, and—yes—in local genius and local mindlessness both. If his reasons were sexual, I realized I'd feel even better about them than I did about where my fears were taking me—or, really, had already taken me.

With his big smile, Peytor said, "I'm probably going to get in trouble for this. But this is what I like doing. New things. Interesting things." His dull yellow hair swung as he stepped forward.

"That is why this is such a good station for you. You have a master who is—more or less—sympathetic with such desires."

For the same reasons, it occurs to me now, it's a good home for me to stop in as I move through the world. But would it be as a good a home if I were confined to it as Peytor is by society and want? Likewise, would being loose and unsupported in the world, without diplomatic missions or my wealth, connections, three trunks of traveling clothes, and ways to transport and support them, be any good for him?

I don't know if he was really listening. Or what he was thinking. But I know he said, "Remember to let me know when they're ready." Perhaps he was interested in showing that he was learning. By that point, however, I was not paying attention any longer. Behind my own smile, I was dwelling on the moment of fear that was, in truth, only now ebbing.

"May I go now, sir?"

"Yes. Certainly, of course." Of course he had picked up on the failing interest of a momentarily enthusiastic master. Yet I felt guilt that it had failed.

"Now, don't forget, I'll have several sets to be washed—if you want to wash them—in a few days. I change them every—" and stopped because I realized that was none of his business. Though— perhaps as someone interested in washing them, he was curious to know why I wore them, since neither he—nor anyone else who worked in the house, I was certain—did. Servants didn't. He got up, said "Thank you, sir . . . ?" with far too much curiosity for a good servant to show at a master's sudden preoccupation or eccentricity.

After an hour, I was sure I'd found our conversation far more instructive than he could have (all he could have learned is how to say, a bit more clearly, what he knew of his own life), though I still fancied him happy as he limped from my room.

"Would you like me to put a shovel of coals in the warming pan and run them under your sheets?"

"No. No. That really isn't necessary."

So he opened the door—hesitated a moment with the false certainty of someone who'd thought hours about asking this question, and who, on deciding to ask it no matter what, realizes on its threshold that he still is unsure—and with one hand on the door handle behind him, demanded, low and hurried, though I'm sure he'd hoped to sound self-assured and somehow professional, "Could I . . . can I take your . . . *perruque* with me, and clean and . . . put new powder on it, perhaps. Brush it . . . ?" He added quickly, "I'll have it back in an hour!"

Oh, I thought. He's one of *those*. "No," I said. "You may not." But then, so am I.

Hastily, he backed out and closed the door. As was appropriate, neither of us had said good night. But I sat wondering why I had been so eager for him to like me and so anxious that he might not.

Even more, why, when I'd thought about asking him what might have happened to him in the country, had I had a moment's terror, as if he hated me?

It had destroyed most of my pleasure in the conversation.

From the side of the fireplace, I took one of the pans by its handle. The padded brocade was neutral in temperature. But my thumb on top and my fore knuckle underneath lay on the metal band at its edge. The metal was cold.

Could he have intuited that I might have been thinking that he who'd said he wanted to wash my smallclothes actually wanted to kill me and . . . yes, eat me like a cannibal?

And I felt—after today's revelation—as if this were a rational possibility, which was the *most* frightening thing about it!

My heart beat hard again, though as I breathed deeper I could see myself as funny, as ridiculous, as absurd—a new word arriving in my mind with each pounding in my chest . . .

I leaned the warming pan back against the stone, and turned away from the coal shovel on its rack with the fire tongues. My penance would be to sleep in a cold bed. (Maybe I should have tried some of Gunter's salts.) Besides, isn't half the work people are always commending me for done simply because I'm very lazy and want to make everything in the world easier for all?

But thoughts, in such ferment, do not cease. Though humor came to overlay the fear, it did not displace it. Was this the way aristocratic guilt, or any other kind, could turn into simple insanity? Or was it an inescapable risk faced by anyone who thinks as I do? Might a peasant feel it as much as a prince? Everyone has seen crazy peasants loose in the countryside. Many attics of dukes or barons held their family embarrassments, young or ancient, in townhouses or country manors, chained in bare stone rooms or locked in padded chambers with the food and the slop pots removed or replaced far too infrequently for either health or comfort, the inhabitants wanting to eat or fearing being eaten— or worse. I knew of several such families.

I reached up and worked a middle finger under the wig's cloth band around my all-but-shaved pate, and pulled so that the paste that held the false hair in place tugged loose, stinging across my head. (I could hear the skin tearing free.) I looked for the bust on which to set it down. In just two days the tasseled cloth on which the wooden statue sat would be faintly ringed with powder.

Next time I see him, I *must* ask if anyone ever ate anyone he knew—in the *rampjaar*.

Or before it or after it.

Or if he had.

The truth is not just a pleasant field to work in. It can free you from real terror. Especially when the choice is between the terror of asking and the greater terror of not knowing if such a fate lies lurking for you.

And I must go on to ask, had he cleaned shit off water-closet walls before he came inside? And how did he feel about it? Precisely such questions (as much as why more than a dozen men and women in an enraged mob ate from the bodies of two murdered aristocrats), finally, made that Jew's *Tractatus Theologico-Politicus*, which I'd first read half a dozen years before, and reread—I confess, though for many people it would be confessing to a terrible crime—twice since. (Once, ironically enough, in Hamburg, and once here in Amsterdam, two years ago, when I wouldn't have considered coming to see the man I'd—almost—snuck off to see today.)

I got up, moved the lamp from stone mantel to inlaid table, and stripped off my clothing, hanging some things on the polished wooden clothes racks in the closet, putting my smallclothes, yes, in a pile at the back to give—in days—to Peytor.

Rather think such horrors, such possibilities, were the concerns of Jews and peasants in The Hague. Certainly rather that than believe such things could infiltrate the Amsterdam home of my longstanding university friend, so generous to diplomatic scions like me and deformed peasants like Peytor—and trust he had an eye, a feel, a sense for those of us who were . . . good? (And could gullible Gunter have such a sense of anything . . . ?) I wished I might hear a church bell, as I had that afternoon when I'd left the Jew's. But more and more they ring the bell less and less after sundown in cities. It's not like the country with distance and tradition to dull such night disturbances. I wanted to hear it because it reminded me of the country. And, I realized, right then, the country was no longer safe.

Drifting out of my sensory past into language, I remembered he'd had a slight smell, different from the ordinary outside men who come into the house now and again for a few minutes to carry a message, work for an hour, or stop in the scullery and chat with a kitchen woman.

It was Cologne water, I think.

I remembered when, as Gunter had prepared to step from his carriage that morning at his Jew's, I'd thought he was showing me his hands because they held no weapon. Was Peytor the dirk he might have gripped? Was Spinoza? Was I to be the victim of either, because of my sympathies for both?

I've been so taken up with these dialectical musings I haven't been able to note that I've now arranged two other visits in the city for my duke. Yes, one more to The Hague to see another . . . lens maker, Leeuwenhoek, who is *not* a Jew. For a mad moment, that fact seemed as much a relief as if I'd learned that the lame boy who'd wanted to wash my underthings and brush out my wig was not a cannibal! As eager as Peytor is to advance himself, I will manage, once those visits are done, to go back to Spinoza for at least another day or even two. And I'm *not* going to give him the calculator: that's a gift for London. I jot this down just to get my mind off the horror. The brilliant hermit at Trinity and I, at least, are destined to be friends.

Or had I learned that he might be—

Peytor's master wears Cologne too—as do I. At this point in my life, in the day, in history, the liberal use of that scent strikes me as a sign. Its meaning is ambiguous and will remain so—until I run into it on another peasant, perhaps . . . ?

And do you know? That was the beginning of my most terrifying night in Amsterdam, though nothing happened but the rising and falling of my own fears of Peytor's unannounced return. What calmed them, finally, as we neared a dark, drizzly dawn, during which he never came, was that I realized that whether he'd learned he might dab on some Cologne water to alter the way people thought of him (though not necessarily in the way he wished)—with or without Mary's help, wherever she was that evening—I was probably as safe as I could have been, if only because the night was over, and I was still there.

But there were still more visits.

Racism and Science Fiction

RACISM FOR ME HAS always appeared to be first and foremost a system, largely supported by material and economic conditions at work in a field of social traditions. Thus, though racism is always made manifest through individuals' decisions, actions, words, and feelings, when we have the luxury of looking at it with the longer view (and we don't, always), usually I don't see much point in blaming people personally, white or black, for their feelings or even for their specific actions—as long as they remain this side of the criminal. These are not what stabilize the system. These are not what promote and reproduce the system. These are not the points where the most lasting changes can be introduced to alter the system.

For better or for worse, I am often spoken of as the first African-American science fiction writer. But I wear that originary label as uneasily as any writer has worn the label of science fiction itself. Among the ranks of what is often referred to as proto–science fiction, there are a number of black writers. M.P. Shiel, whose *Purple Cloud* and *Lord of the Sea* are still read, was a Creole with some African ancestry. Black leader Martin Delany

(1812–1885—alas, no relation) wrote his single and highly imaginative novel, still to be found on the shelves of Barnes & Noble today, *Blake, or The Huts of America* (1857), about an imagined successful slave revolt in Cuba and the American South—which is about as close to an SF-style alternate history novel as you can get. Other black writers whose work certainly borders on science fiction include Sutton E. Griggs and his novel *Imperio Imperium* (1899) in which an African-American secret society conspires to found a separate black state by taking over Texas, and Edward Johnson, who, following Bellamy's example in *Looking Backward* (1888), wrote *Light Ahead for the Negro* (1904), telling of a black man transported into a socialist United States in the far future. I believe I first heard Harlan Ellison make the point that we know of dozens upon dozens of early pulp writers only as names: They conducted their careers entirely by mail—in a field and during an era when pen-names were the rule rather than the exception. Among the "Remington C. Scotts" and the "Frank P. Joneses" who litter the contents pages of the early pulps, we simply have no way of knowing if one, three, or seven or them—or even many more—were not blacks, Hispanics, women, native Americans, Asians, or whatever. Writing is like that.

Toward the end of the Harlem Renaissance, the black social critic George Schuyler (1895–1977) published an acidic satire *Black No More: Being an Account of the Strange and Wonderful Workings of Science in the Land of the Free, A.D. 1933–1940* (New York: Macaulay Company, 1931), which hinges on a three-day treatment costing fifty dollars through which black people can turn themselves white. The treatment involves "a formidable apparatus of sparkling nickel. It resembled a cross between a dentist chair and an electric chair." The confusion this causes throughout racist America (as well as among black folks themselves) gives Schuyler a chance to satirize both white leaders and black. (Though W.E.B. Du Bois was himself lampooned by Schuyler as the aloof, money-hungry hypocrite Dr. Shakespeare Agamemnon Beard, Du Bois, in his column "The Browsing Reader" [in *The Crisis*, March 1931] called the novel "an extremely significant work" and "a rollicking, keen, good-natured criticism of the Negro problem in the United States" that was bound to be "abundantly misunderstood" because such was the fate of all satire.) The story follows the adventures of the dashing black Max Dasher and his sidekick Bunny, who become white and make their way through a world rendered topsy-turvy by the spreading racial ambiguity and deception. Toward the climax, the two white perpetrators of the system who have made themselves rich on the scheme are lynched by a group of whites (at a place called Happy Hill) who believe the two men are blacks in disguise. Though the term did not exist, here the "humor" becomes so "black" as to take on elements of inchoate American horror. For his scene, Schuyler simply used accounts of actual lynchings of black men at the time, with a few changes in wording:

> The two men . . . were stripped naked, held down
> by husky and willing farm hands and their ears and
> genitals cut off with jackknives. . . . Some wag sewed
> their ears to their backs and they were released to
> run . . . [but were immediately brought down with re-
> volvers by the crowd] amidst the uproarious laughter

of the congregation. . . . [Still living, the two were bound together at a stake while] little boys and girls gaily gathered excelsior, scrap paper, twigs and small branches, while their proud parents fetched logs, boxes, kerosene. . . . [Reverend McPhule said a prayer, the flames were lit, the victims screamed, and the] crowd whooped with glee and Reverend McPhule beamed with satisfaction. . . . The odor of cooking meat permeated the clear, country air and many a nostril was guiltily distended. . . . When the roasting was over, the more adventurous members of Rev. McPhule's flock rushed to the stake and groped in the two bodies for skeletal souvenirs such as forefingers, toes and teeth. Proudly their pastor looked on (217–18).

Might this have been too much for the readers of *Amazing* and *Astounding*? As it does for many black folk today, such a tale, despite the '30s pulp diction, has a special place for me. Among the family stories I grew up with, one was an account of a similar lynching of a cousin of mine from only a decade or so before the year in which Schuyler's story is set. Even the racial ambiguity of Schuyler's victims speaks to the story. A woman who looked white, my cousin was several months pregnant and traveling with her much darker husband when they were set upon by white men (because they believed the marriage was miscegenous) and lynched in a manner equally gruesome: Her husband's body was similarly mutilated. And her child was no longer in her body when their corpses, as my father recounted the incident to me in the '40s, were returned in a wagon to the campus of the black episcopal college where my grandparents were administrators. Hundreds on hundreds of such social murders were recorded in detail by witnesses and participants between the Civil War and the Second World War. Thousands on thousands more went unrecorded. (Billy the Kid claimed to have taken active part in a more than half a dozen such murders of "Mexicans, niggers, and injuns," which were not even counted among his famous twenty-one adolescent killings.) But this is (just one of) the horrors from which racism arises—and where it can still all too easily go.

In 1936 and 1938, under the pen name "Samuel I. Brooks," Schuyler had two long stories published in some sixty-three weekly installments in the *Pittsburgh Courier*, a black Pennsylvania newspaper, about a black organization led by a black Dr. Belsidus, who plots to take over the world—work that Schuyler considered "hokum and hack work of the purest vein." Schuyler was known as an extreme political conservative, though the trajectory to that conservatism was very similar to Heinlein's. (Unlike Heinlein's, though, Schuyler's view of science fiction was as conservative as anything about him.) Schuyler's early socialist period was followed by a later conservatism that Schuyler himself, at least, felt in no way harbored any contradiction with his former principles, even though he joined the John Birch Society toward the start of the '60s and wrote for its news organ, *American Opinion*. His second Dr. Belsidus story remained unfinished, and the two were not collected in book form until 1991, fourteen years after his death (*Black Empire*, by George S. Schuyler, eds. Robert A. Hill and Kent Rasmussen, Boston: Northeastern University Press).

Since I began to publish in 1962, I have often been asked, by people of all colors, what my experience of racial prejudice in the science fiction field has been. Has it been nonexistent? By no means: It was definitely there. A child of the political protests of the '50s and '60s, I've frequently said to people who asked that question: As long as there are only one, two, or a handful of us, however, I presume in a field such as science fiction, where many of its writers come out of the liberal-Jewish tradition, prejudice will most likely remain a slight force—until, say, black writers start to number 13, 15, 20 percent of the total. At that point, where the competition might be perceived as having some economic heft, chances are we will have as much racism and prejudice here as in any other field.

We are still a long way away from such statistics.

But we are certainly moving closer.

After—briefly—being my student at the Clarion Science Fiction Writers' Workshop, Octavia Butler entered the field with her first story, "Crossover," in 1971 and her first novel, *Patternmaster*, in 1976—fourteen years after my own first novel appeared in winter of '62. But she recounts her story with brio and insight. Everyone was very glad to see her! After several short story sales, Steven Barnes first came to general attention in 1981 with *Dreampark* and other collaborations with Larry Niven. Charles Saunders published his *Imaro* novels with DAW Books in the early '80s. Even more recently in the collateral field of horror, Tananarive Due has published *The Between* (1996) and *My Soul to Keep* (1997). Last year all of us except Charles were present at the first African-American science fiction writers' conference sponsored by Clark Atlanta University, called the African-American Fantastic Imagination. This year Toronto-based writer Nalo Hopkinson (another Clarion student whom I have the pleasure of being able to boast of as having also taught at Clarion) published her award-winning SF novel *Brown Girl in the Ring* (New York: Warner, 1998). Another black North American writer is Haitian-born Claude-Michel Prévost, a francophone writer who publishes out of Vancouver, British Columbia. Since people ask me regularly what examples of prejudice have I experienced in the science fiction field, I thought this might be the time to answer, then—with a tale.

With five days to go in my twenty-fourth year, on March 25, 1967, my sixth science fiction novel, *Babel-17*, won a Nebula Award (a tie, actually) from the Science Fiction Writers of America. That same day the first copies of my eighth, *The Einstein Intersection*, became available at my publishers' office. (Because of publishing schedules, my seventh, *Empire Star*, had preceded the sixth into print the previous spring.) At home on my desk at the back of an apartment I shared on St. Mark's Place, my ninth, *Nova*, was a little more than three months from completion.

On February 10, a month and a half before the March awards, in its partially completed state *Nova* had been purchased by Doubleday & Co. Three months after the awards banquet, in June, when it was done, with that first Nebula under my belt, I submitted *Nova* for serialization to the famous SF editor of *Analog* magazine, John W. Campbell Jr. He rejected it, with a note and phone call to my agent explaining that he didn't feel his readership would be able to relate to a black main character. That was one of my first direct encounters, as a professional writer, with the slippery and always commercialized form of liberal

American prejudice: Campbell had nothing against my being black, you understand. (There reputedly exists a letter from him to horror writer Dean Koontz, from only a year or two later, in which Campbell argues in all seriousness that a technologically advanced black civilization is a social and a biological impossibility.) No, perish the thought! Surely there was not a prejudiced bone in his body! It's just that I had, by pure happenstance, chosen to write about someone whose mother was from Senegal (and whose father was from Norway), and it was the poor benighted readers, out there in America's heartland, who, in 1967, would be too upset . . .

It was all handled as though I'd just happened to have dressed my main character in a purple brocade dinner jacket. (In the phone call Campbell made it fairly clear that this was his only reason for rejecting the book. Otherwise he rather liked it.) Purple brocade just wasn't big with the buyers that season. Sorry . . .

Today if something like that happened, I would probably give the information to those people who feel it their job to make such things as widely known as possible. At the time, however, I swallowed it—a mark of how the times, and I, have changed. I told myself I was too busy writing. The most profitable trajectory for a successful science fiction novel in those days was for an SF book to start life as a magazine serial, move on to hardcover publication, and finally be reprinted as a mass market paperback. If you were writing a novel a year (or, say, three novels every two years, which was then almost what I was averaging), that was the only way to push your annual income up, at the time, from four to five figures—and the low five figures at that. That was the point I began to realize I probably was not going to be able to make the kind of living (modest enough!) that, only a few months before, at the awards banquet, I'd let myself envision. The things I saw myself writing in the future, I already knew, were going to be more rather than less controversial. The percentage of purple brocade was only going to go up.

The second installment of my story here concerns the first time the word "Negro" was said to me, as a direct reference to my racial origins, by someone in the science fiction community. Understand that, since the late '30s, that community, that world had been largely Jewish, highly liberal, and with notable exceptions leaned well to the left. Even its right-wing mavens, Robert Heinlein or Poul Anderson (or, indeed, Campbell), would have far preferred to go to a leftist party and have a friendly argument with some smart socialists than actually to hang out with the right-wing and libertarian organizations which they may well have supported on principle and, in Heinlein's case, with donations. April 14, 1968, a year and—perhaps—three weeks later, was the evening of the next Nebula Awards Banquet. A fortnight before, I had turned twenty-six. That year my eighth novel, *The Einstein Intersection* (which had materialized as an object on the day of the previous year's), and my short story, "Aye, and Gomorrah . . ." were both nominated.

In those days the Nebula banquet was a black-tie affair with upward of a hundred guests at a midtown hotel-restaurant. Quite incidentally, it was a time of upheaval and uncertainty in my personal life (which, I suspect, is tantamount to saying I was a twenty-six-year-old writer). But that evening my mother and sister and a friend, as well as my wife, were at my table. My novel won—and the presentation of the glittering Lucite trophy was followed by a discomforting speech from an eminent member of SFWA.

Perhaps you've heard such disgruntled talks. They begin, as did this one, "What I have to say tonight, many of you are not going to like . . ." and went on to castigate the organization for letting itself be taken in by (the phrase was, or was something very like) "pretentious literary nonsense," unto granting it awards, and abandoning the old values of good, solid, craftsman-like storytelling. My name was not mentioned, but it was evident that I was (along with Roger Zelazny, not present) the prime target of this fusillade. It's an odd experience, I must tell you, to accept an award from a hall full of people in tuxedos and evening gowns and then, from the same podium at which you accepted it, hear a half-hour jeremiad from an éminence grise declaring that award to be worthless and the people who voted it to you duped fools. It's not paranoia. By count I caught more than a dozen sets of eyes sweeping between me and the speaker going on about the triviality of work such as mine and the foolishness of the hundred-plus writers who had voted for it.

As you might imagine, the applause was slight, uncomfortable, and scattered. There was more coughing and chair scraping than clapping. By the end of the speech, I was drenched with the tricklings of mortification and wondering what I'd done to deserve them. The master of ceremonies, Robert Silverberg, took the podium and said, "Well, I guess we've all been put in our place." There was a bitter chuckle. And the next award was announced.

It again went to me—for my short story "Aye, and Gomorrah . . ." I had, by that time, forgotten it was in the running. For the second time that evening I got up and went to the podium to accept my trophy (it sits on a shelf above my desk about two feet away from me as I write), but, in dazzled embarrassment, it occurred to me as I was walking to the front of the hall that I must say something in my defense, though mistily I perceived it had best be as indirect as the attack. With my sweat-soaked undershirt beneath my formal turtleneck peeling and unpeeling from my back at each step, I took the podium and my second trophy of the evening. Into the microphone I said, as calmly as I could manage: "I write the novels and stories that I do and work on them as hard as I can to make them the best I can. That you've chosen to honor them—and twice in one night—is warming. Thank you."

I received a standing ovation—though I was aware it was as much in reaction to the upbraiding of the naysayer as it was in support of anything I had done. I walked back down toward my seat, but as I passed one of the tables, a woman agent (not my own) who had several times written me and been supportive of my work, took my arm as I went by and pulled me down to say, "That was elegant, Chip . . . !" while the applause continued. At the same time, I felt a hand on my other sleeve—on the arm that held the Lucite block of the Nebula itself—and I turned to Isaac Asimov (whom I'd met for the first time at the banquet the year before), sitting on the other side and now pulling me toward him. With a large smile, wholly saturated with evident self-irony, he leaned toward me to say: "You know, Chip, we only voted you those awards because you're Negro . . . !" (This was

1968; the term "black" was not yet common parlance.) I smiled back (there was no possibility he had intended the remark in any way seriously—as anything other than an attempt to cut through the evening's many tensions . . . Still, part of me rolled my eyes silently to heaven and said: Do I really need to hear this right at this moment?) and returned to my table.

The way I read his statement then, and the way I read it today; indeed, anything else would be a historical misreading, is that Ike was trying to use a self-evidently tasteless absurdity (he was famous for them) to defuse some of the considerable anxiety in the hall that night; it is a standard male trope, needless to say. I think he was trying to say that race probably took little or no part in his or any of the other writers' minds who had voted for me.

But such ironies cut in several directions. I don't know whether Asimov realized he was saying this as well, but as an old historical materialist, if only as an afterthought, he must have realized that he was saying too: No one here will ever look at you, read a word your write, or consider you in any situation, no matter whether the roof is falling in or the money is pouring in, without saying to him- or herself (whether in an attempt to count it or to discount it), "Negro . . ." The racial situation, permeable as it might sometimes seem (and it is, yes, highly permeable), is nevertheless your total surround. Don't you ever forget it . . . ! And I never have.

The fact that this particular "joke" emerged just then, at that most anxiety-torn moment, when the only-three-year-old, volatile organization of feisty science fiction writers saw itself under a virulent battering from internal conflicts over shifting aesthetic values, meant that, though the word had not yet been said to me or written about me till then, it had clearly inhered in every step and stage of my then just-six years as a professional writer. And from then on, it was, interestingly, written regularly, though I did not in any way change my own self-presentation. Judy Merril had already referred to me in print as "a handsome Negro." James Blish would soon write of me as "a merry Negro." (I mean, can you imagine anyone at the same time writing of "a merry Jew"?)

Here the story takes a sanguine turn.

The man who'd made the speech had apparently not yet actually read my nominated novel when he wrote his talk. He had merely had it described to him by a friend, a notoriously eccentric reader, who had fulminated that the work was clearly and obviously beneath consideration as a serious science fiction novel: Each chapter began with a set of quotes from literary texts that had nothing to do with science at all! Our naysayer had gone along with this evaluation, at least as far as putting together his rebarbative speech.

When, a week or two later, he decided to read the book for himself (in case he was challenged on specifics), he found, to his surprise, he liked it—and, from what embarrassment I can only guess, became one of my staunchest and most articulate supporters, as an editor and a critic. (A lesson about reading here: Do your share, and you can save yourself and others a lot of embarrassment.) And *Nova*, after its Doubleday appearance in '68 and some pretty stunning reviews, garnered what was then a record advance for an SF novel paid to date by Bantam Books (a record broken shortly thereafter), ushering in the twenty years when I could actually support myself (almost) by writing alone.

(Algis J. Budrys, who also had been there that evening, wrote in his January '69 review in *Galaxy*, "Samuel R. Delany, right now, as of this book, *Nova*, not as of some future book or some accumulated body of work, is the best science fiction writer in the world, at a time when competition for that status is intense. I don't see how a science fiction writer can do more than wring your heart while telling you how it works. No writer can." Even then I knew enough not to take such hyperbole seriously. I mention it to suggest the pressures around against which one had to keep one's head straight—and, yes, to brag just a little. But it's that desire to have it both ways—to realize it's meaningless, but to take some straited pleasure nevertheless from the fact that, at least, somebody was inspired to say it—that defines the field in which the dangerous slippages in your reality picture start, slippages that lead to that monstrous and insufferable egotism so ugly in so many much-praised artists.)

But what Asimov's quip also tells us is that, for any black artist (and you'll forgive me if I stick to the nomenclature of my young manhood, that my friends and contemporaries, appropriating it from Dr. Du Bois, fought to set in place, breaking into libraries through the summer of '68 and taking down the signs saying Negro Literature and replacing them with signs saying "black literature"—the small "b" on "black" is a very significant letter, an attempt to ironize and de-transcendentalize the whole concept of race, to render it provisional and contingent, a significance that many young people today, white and black, who lackadaisically capitalize it, have lost track of), the concept of race informed everything about me, so that it could surface—and did surface—precisely at those moments of highest anxiety, a manifesting brought about precisely by the white gaze, if you will, whenever it turned, discommoded for whatever reason, in my direction. Some have asked if I perceived my entrance into science fiction as a transgression.

Certainly not at the entrance point, in any way. But it's clear from my story, I hope (and I have told many others about that fraught evening), transgression inheres, however unarticulated, in every aspect of the black writer's career in America. That it emerged in such a charged moment is, if anything, only to be expected in such a society as ours. How could it be otherwise?

A question that I am asked nowhere near as frequently—and the recounting of tales such as the above tends to obviate and, as it were, put to sleep—is the question: If that was the first time you were aware of direct racism, when was the last time?

To live in the United States as a black man or woman, the fact is the answer to that question is rarely other than: A few hours ago, a few days, a few weeks . . . So, my hypothetical interlocutor persists, when is the last time you were aware of racism in the science fiction field per se. Well, I would have to say, last weekend I just spent attending Readercon 10, a fine and rich convention of concerned and alert people, a wonderful and stimulating convocation of high-level panels and quality programming, with, this year, almost a hundred professionals, some dozen of whom were editors and the rest of whom were writers.

In the dealers' room was an Autograph Table where, throughout the convention, pairs of writers were assigned an hour each to make themselves available for book signing. The hours the writers would be at the table were part of the program. At 12:30

on Saturday I came to sit down just as Nalo Hopkinson came to join me.

Understand, on a personal level, I could not be more de-lighted to sign with Nalo. My student years ago, she is charming and talented, and today I think of her as a friend. We both en-joyed our hour together. That is not in question. After our hour was up, however, and we went and had some lunch together with her friend David, we both found ourselves more amused than not that the two black American SF writers at Readercon, out of nearly eighty professionals, had ended up at the autograph table in the same hour. Let me repeat: I don't think you can have rac-ism as a positive system until you have that socioeconomic sup-port suggested by that (rather arbitrary) 20 percent/80 percent proportion. But what racism as a system does is isolate and seg-regate the people of one race, or group, or ethnos from another. As a system it can be fueled by chance as much as by hostility or by the best of intentions. ("I thought they would be more comfortable together. I thought they would want to be with each other . . .") And certainly one of its strongest manifestations is as a socio-visual system in which people become used to always seeing blacks with other blacks and so—because people are used to it—being uncomfortable whenever they see blacks mixed in, at whatever proportion, with whites.

My friend of a decade's standing, Eric Van, had charge at this year's Readercon of the programming the coffee klatches, readings, and autograph sessions. One of the goals—facilitated by computer—was not only to assign the visiting writers to the panels they wanted to be on, but to try, when possible, not to schedule those panels when other panels the same writers wanted to hear were also scheduled. This made some tight windows. I called Eric after the con, who kindly pulled up grids and sched-ule sheets on his computer. "Well," he said, "lots of writers, of course, asked to sign together. But certainly neither you nor Nalo did that. As I recall, Nalo had a particularly tight schedule. She wasn't arriving until late Friday night. Saturday at 12:30 was pretty much the only time she could sign—so, of the two of you, she was scheduled first. When I consulted the grid, the first two names that came up who were free at the same time were you and Jonathan Lethem. You came first in the alphabet, so I put you down. I remember looking at the two of you, you and Nalo, and saying, 'Well, certainly there's nothing wrong with that pairing.' But the point is, I wasn't thinking along racial lines. I probably should have been more sensitive to the possible racial implications—"

Let me reiterate: Racism is a system. As such, it is fueled as much by chance as by hostile intentions and equally the best intentions as well. It is whatever systematically acclimates people, of all colors, to become comfortable with the isolation and segregation of the races, on a visual, social, or economic level—which in turn supports and is supported by socioeconomic discrimination. Because it is a system, however, I believe personal guilt is almost never the proper response in such a situation. Certainly, personal guilt will never replace a bit of well-founded systems analysis. And one does not have to be a particularly inventive science fiction writer to see a time, when we are much closer to that 20 percent division, where we black writers all hang out together, sign our books together, have our separate tracks of programming, if we don't have our own segregated conventions, till we just never bother to show up at yours because we make you uncomfortable and you don't really want us; and you make us feel the same way . . .

One fact that adds its own shadowing to the discussion is the attention that has devolved on Octavia Butler since her most-deserved 1995 receipt of a MacArthur "genius" award. But the interest has largely been articulated in terms of interest in "African-American Science Fiction," whether it be among the halls of MIT, where Butler and I appeared last, or the University of Chicago, where we are scheduled to appear together in a few months. Now Butler is a gracious, intelligent, and wonderfully impressive writer. But if she were a jot less great-hearted than she is, she may very well wonder, "Why, when you invite me, do you always invite that guy, Delany?"

The fact is, while it is always a personal pleasure to appear with her, Butler and I are very different writers, interested in very different things. And because I am the one who benefits by this highly artificial generalization of the literary interest in Butler's work into this in-many-ways-artificial interest in African-American science fiction (I'm not the one who won the MacArthur, after all), I think it's incumbent upon me to be the one publicly to question it. And while it provides generous honoraria for us both, I think that the nature of the generalization (since we have an extraordinarily talented black woman SF writer, why don't we generalize that interest to all black SF writers, male and female?) has elements of both racism and sexism about it.

One other thing allows me to question it in this manner. Last year at the African-American science fiction conference at Clark Atlanta University, where, with Steve Barnes and Tananarive Due, Butler and I met with each other, talked and exchanged conversation and ideas, spoke and interacted with the university students and teachers and the other writers in that historic black university, all of us present had the kind of rich and lively experience that was much more likely to forge common interests and that, indeed, at a later date could easily leave shared themes in our subsequent work. This aware and vital meeting to respond specifically to black youth in Atlanta is not, however, what usually occurs at an academic presentation in a largely white university doing an evening on African-American SF. Butler and I, born and raised on opposite sides of the country, half a dozen years apart, share many of the experiences of racial exclusion and the familial and social responses to that exclusion which constitute a race. But as long a racism functions as a system, it is still fueled from aspects of the perfectly laudable desires of interested whites to observe this thing, however dubious its reality, that exists largely by means of its having been named: African-American science fiction.

To pose a comparison of some heft:

In the days of cyberpunk, I was often cited by both the writers involved and the critics writing about them as an influence. As a critic, several times I wrote about the cyberpunk writers. And Bill Gibson wrote a gracious and appreciative introduction to the 1996 reprint of my novel *Dhalgren*. Thus you might think that there were a fair number of reasons for me to appear on panels with those writers or to be involved in programs with them. With all the attention that has come to her in the last years, Butler has been careful (and accurate) in not claiming that I am any sort of influence on her. I have never written specifically about her work. Nor, as far as I know, has she ever mentioned me in print.

Nevertheless, throughout all of cyberpunk's active history, I only recall being asked to sit on one cyberpunk panel with Bill, and that was largely a media-focused event at the Kennedy Center. In the last ten years, however, I have been invited to appear with Octavia at least six times, with another appearance scheduled in a few months and a joint interview with the both of us scheduled for a national magazine. All the comparison points out is the pure and unmitigated strength of the discourse of race in our country vis-à-vis any other. In a society such as ours, the discourse of race is so involved and embraided with the discourse of racism that I would defy anyone ultimately and authoritatively to distinguish them in any absolute manner once and for all.

Well, then, how does one combat racism in science fiction, even in such a nascent form as it might be fibrillating, here and there? The best way is to build a certain social vigilance into the system—and that means into conventions such as Readercon: Certainly racism in its current and sometimes difficult form becomes a good topic for panels. Because race is a touchy subject, in situations such as the above mentioned Readercon autographing session where chance and propinquity alone threw blacks together, you simply ask: Is this all right, or are there other people that, in this case, you would rather be paired with for whatever reason—even if that reason is only for breaking up the appearance of possible racism; since the appearance of possible racism can be just as much a factor in reproducing and promoting racism as anything else: Racism is as much about accustoming people to becoming used to certain racial configurations so that they are specifically not used to others, as it is about anything else. Indeed, we have to remember that what we are combating is called prejudice: prejudice is prejudgment—in this case, the prejudgment that the way things just happen to fall out are "all right," when there well may be reasons for setting them up otherwise. Editors and writers need to be alerted to the socioeconomic pressure on such gathering social groups to reproduce inside a new system by the virtue of "outside pressures." Because we still live in a racist society, the only way to combat it in any systematic way is to establish—and repeatedly revamp—antiracist institutions and traditions. That means actively encouraging the attendance of nonwhite readers and writers at conventions. It means actively presenting nonwhite writers with a forum to discuss precisely these problems in the con programming. (It seems absurd to have to point out that racism is by no means exhausted simply by black/white differences: indeed, one might argue that it is only touched on here.) And it means encouraging dialogue among, and encouraging intermixing with, the many sorts of writers who make up the SF community.

It means supporting those traditions.

I've already started discussing this with Eric. I will be going on to speak about it with the next year's programmers.

Readercon is certainly as good a place as any, not to start but to continue.

Editorial Postscript

Since its first publication almost two decades ago, "Racism and Science Fiction" has become a classic in and out of the field. Asked if there is anything he would add or alter today (2017), the author answered:

Not really. I said in the essay that when the numbers of black writers, women writers, gay writers, Asian writers reach a high enough recognizable proportion to start having economic heft, then there would be social divisions along those social lines. And now there are. That's not, as they say, rocket science.

"Discourse in an Older Sense"
Samuel R. Delany interviewed by Terry Bisson

You recently completed a novel, Through the Valley of the Nest of Spiders, *almost as long, every bit as challenging, and seemingly as ambitious as* Dhalgren. *What's it about? Isn't the "Great American Novel" a young writer's game?*

Well, it was published on my 70th birthday and, yes, was celebrated with a conference, Delany at 70, at the University of Maryland. But—paradoxically—it was published by a very small press (Donald Weise's Magnus Books) that never seemed to have copies available over the next few years. Thus are the paradoxes of achieving age and what may (or may not) be artistic maturity (or the old-age dodderings of an artist who has gone on babbling long past the time he might have done better to shut up because he's only destroying his—or her—own reputation: which are certainly many of us) in a marginal genre in this age.

It's about two working-class garbagemen, one from the area, one transplanted from the big city in Atlanta, who meet, become lovers, and live and work on the Georgia coast together for the rest of their lives.

It's got a lot of what I learned about relationships from the twenty years I'd been with Dennis, and the eight years I'd been with Frank Romeo—and even the thirteen years I'd been with Marilyn Hacker.

As well, I got the same thousand-dollar advance for this 804-page novel as I got for my first 148-page book, *The Jewels of Aptor*, back in 1961. Now, consider the inflation over those fifty years. Or the fact that this was the first novel I'd called "science fiction" in thirty years, though I'd published a number—including *Hogg*, *The Mad Man*, and the series Return to Nevèrÿon that a number of critics think is my best work (its actual worth I don't know and can't know, even if you try to tell me)—in between time that had made me more money, certainly.

You dedicated your Paris Review *interview to the late Joanna Russ (1937–2011). Were you friends? Why was she, is she, important to you? (I'm writing this query on her birthday.)*

She was a brilliant writer at the sentence level. She was a brilliant thinker at the social level—and she was a great believer in doing everything from an oppositional stance, as well. Yes, we had a great deal of simpatico from the first time we met at Terry Carr's for dinner, during which she didn't tell me she had just finished a novel that I would receive in galleys in only a few weeks: *Picnic on Paradise* (a.k.a. *Picnic in Paradise,* Russ's original title). Friends? Well, we never saw a great deal of one another, but for more than a decade we had a correspondence that reached Victorian proportions. Yes, I think of her as my friend, though there were moments when I strained that friendship.

What's the source of "The Atheist in the Attic?" I know you are a scholar of literary history, but this seems a little off that grid.

Not really (my answer to both implied statements: I'm "not a scholar" and it's "off the grid" only in terms of which grid you mean). Spinoza is the philosopher whose name lurks behind *Through the Valley of the Nest of Spiders*. Eric struggles with reading him, there on the coast of Georgia, for many years. (I remember rereading *Ethica* in my doctor's office for an in-office procedure where a microwave generator was shoved up my butt to take care of my enlarged prostate, a couple of years before I came down with actual prostate cancer.) I struggled too, though I had a whole library of auxiliary readings to help me. From that auxiliary reading, the Nadler and the Bennett and the Stuart Hampshire, and the various anthologies that were once in my very threatened library along with Wiki online—I managed to put together that very small and slight novella, during a very fraught time in my life, just before my library was finally lost . . . or at any rate mostly rendered inaccessible.

I used my own struggles with the text over several years as the fictive basis for Eric's on the Georgia coast—with the difference that I had not promised any transgender black seminarian that I would persevere through three readings the way Eric did in order to hook him on the experience. "Did I succeed in creating a believable fiction?" and "For what percentage of my readers?" are questions I will never know the answers to.

Kim Stanley Robinson often compares historical fiction with Fantasy and SF, in that in both you have to create as well as populate a world. Do you find similarities in the two genres as well?

Yes. And the further away in time you get in both cases, the more the discursive differences have to be faked. These are genres in which nothing can be real except by accident, though reality it still the aesthetic effect you are trying for.

You are considered one of the members of SF's "New Wave." Were you ever part of the London crowd?

On a couple of occasions, in the mid-1960s: for my first visit to Europe, which ended with a trip to London, and my second trip over the subsequent Christmas and New Year's, to stay with John Brunner; and then again in the 1970s, when I actually moved to London for a couple of years, when my daughter was born in Queen Charlotte's Maternity Hospital in Hammersmith, where I was a more or less interested visitor, and where I did my last rewrite of *Dhalgren* and wrote *Trouble on Triton*, before coming home pretty much permanently for many years. But paradoxically, I never considered myself a part of the London SF crowd. I was there because my wife had asked me to come, and her own relation to that crowd was somewhat problematic.

Your debut novel, The Jewels of Aptor, *was postapocalyptic and also ecclesiastical in its way. Was* A Canticle for Leibowitz *an influence? Or was atomic disaster just in the air in those days?*

From Hiroshima through the Cuban Missile Crisis and beyond, atomic war was a pervasive fear in this country. It was what the "Cold War" was about. (Full disclosure: I always found *A Canticle for Leibowitz* all but unreadable.)

Many people now assume it's under control, though some of the reported behavior of our current popular minority president makes it seem still a possibility. Often, it's only after the fact that we know for sure when such crises (have) happen(ed).

You wrote a critical appreciation of SF, The Jewel-Hinged Jaw. *I wrote the cover copy (!) on the first edition back in the 1970s, but I can't recall what the title signified.*

Not the first hardcover edition, but the first paperback edition (David's own very small company, Dragon Press, published a hardcover edition before you got to it at Berkley Books)—and I remember it well. It was the smartest cover copy I'd yet had on a paperback book, and I told David Hartwell to thank you personally for it. For one thing, you'd read the book. That put you notably ahead of most paperback copywriters, at least those who had anything to do with science fiction.

I remember when you came out of the back office and we first said hello to each other, in the office.

The title was not explained in the book. You just had to recognize it. It was from a line in Thomas M. Disch's *Camp Concentration*: from Sacchetti's poem, "The Hierodule," when Disch describes the black idol of language/knowledge/art, which is presumably supposed to speak the truth:

Behold! Behold the black, ungrainèd flesh,
The jaw's jeweled hinge that we can barely glimpse . . .

So, no, you probably didn't and don't recall what the title signified, unless you've been rereading Disch's novel with your literary antennae alert to explaining precisely that conundrum.

In the standard bildungsroman, the young artist lights out from the provinces for London or Paris. You took a subway to Washington Square and Greenwich Village, and then moved into the Lower East Side (alphabet city and the East Village) because the Village proper was too expensive. What was the appeal?

When I was thirteen or fourteen and not sure whether I was going to be a writer or a musician, or even what kind of musician—a folk singer or a composer of serious, avant-garde music—I was drawn to the Village like so many others, as a place where it would be easier to experiment with art and sexuality both.

Washington Square looked entirely different. The fountain and the layout of the park and the restrooms were entirely other from what they are today, and kids came down to the square on the weekend. There was already a bohemian tradition associated with the area, and had been one since the whole thing was an ethnic Italian neighborhood, with its coffee shops and New York University and bookstores and experimental off-off-Broadway theaters.

So did Tompkins Square.

You and the poet Marilyn Hacker have had a lifelong relationship. How did that begin?

We met on our very first day of high school, at the Bronx High School of Science Annex Building, at the other end of the city.

We were friends from then on. My parents had sent me to the Dalton School (and before that Horace Mann–Lincoln) in the center of the city on the east side. But soon we were on that axis that ran through the city—and Marilyn had gotten an early admission into NYU and hadn't liked it; so I went to City College, after my father died and I had managed to graduate from Bronx Science without showing up for my high school graduation.

Like any other life, it was a combination of personal forces, neighborhood forces, and larger forces that are always easier to read after the fact than before.

I had a condition that I didn't even have word for until my wife discovered it in an article when we were both twenty-one: dyslexia.

The dyslexia is part of a larger condition that my daughter—who is a doctor—only explained to me some months ago: Adult Attention Deficit Disorder (AADD). There are drugs for it that I've never tried because I never knew I had it until relatively recently. I spoke to a good friend who has a form of the latter and discovered that he'd tried the drug—which is speed—and hadn't liked the effect, so he'd discontinued it. Since I am twenty years older than he is, would I have the same reaction? I simply don't know.

In the Imaginary Index to Delany, *published by Tyndale House in 2011, there is no entry for Dr. Johnson. What's your beef with the Old Tory?*

First, I've never heard of Tyndale House's *Imaginary Index to Delany*—so I imagine you're making a joke.

Let's just say that I imagined that I was. I was interested in your opinion of Samuel Johnson. Your opinion of his opinions.

I've written about Johnson and recently prepared an essay for a new collection (or rather a letter-essay), where I discussed him and his refutation of Bishop Berkeley, by—rather notoriously—kicking a rock. One of the things I have written, however, is that there is so much knowledge available today that there can be no such thing anymore as a classical education that we can expect more than a relatively few people to share.

Some people's information is other people's misinformation and even disinformation. That is pretty much the contemporary condition. When we say that the same forces that put Obama in office also put Trump in office, eight years later, but at work on a very differently structured political field, what exactly are we saying?

Larry McCaffrey and other critics claim that your Return to Nevèrÿon series "undercut[s] the premises" of the genre [sword and sorcery]. That sounds sort of sneaky. What about your more academic treatises and lectures?

They become less and less academic as I get older: I try to write as clearly as I can. But I roam through genres, letters, lectures, interviews, journals, Facebook posts, and various kinds of fictions.

You won a Hugo for an early memoir, The Motion of Light in Water, *about your time as a young, gay writer in the East Village. Then there was your novel,* Dark Reflections, *about an older gay writer walking the same streets. Anything of interest happen in between?*

Interesting to me? Or interesting to readers? Presumably it was interesting enough for me to make whatever effort I needed to write it. The interest of readers—which is the one that finally counts—lies *with* readers. So they're the ones you have to ask.

I believe the éminence grise who excoriated you (and Zelazny) at the '68 Nebula Awards banquet has long since been identified. Can you name names?

Yes, it was Frederik Pohl. And, as I said, shortly he actually *read* the work in question that had inspired him to such ire, and decided—to his surprise, I gather—that he rather liked it in spite of Lester Del Ray's fulminating against it, which is what had convinced him to bad-mouth it sight unseen. (This is supposition on my part. We never discussed it directly.) He started assigning me cover stories—which was a mixed blessing. But they made me a few hundred dollars when it was money I needed. Both "Cage of Brass" and "High Weir" were Pohl cover stories for *If*, the most experimental of what were then known as the Galaxy Combine. A cover story, which is something that almost never happens in the magazines these days, is where the editor has brought one or a number of covers before the story is written, and then shows the cover to the writer and says, okay, write a story to go with this.

A few years after that, Pohl was the editor who bought and published *Dhalgren*. Which is to say, he managed to do a 180-degree turn when it came to judging my work. But the whole SF community was smaller, younger, and things like that could happen.

You are one of the few literary academics in the U.S. without a doctorate. Has that been an impediment or an asset?

To the extent it represents a lot of experiences with the university system I never had, it was an impediment. (I not only don't have a PhD, I never finished more than a term of college. I made two stabs at completing my second term—and couldn't hack it. I wasn't organized enough. That's the ADD that encompassed my dyslexia.) Perhaps to some, it made me look a little more interesting; but then—as I said—you'll have to ask them, not me.

One sentence on each, please: Alan Ansen, George Eliot, Junot Díaz.

Impossible question! But here goes, though I might try for a small paragraph.

Alan Ansen was nice, civilized, and in his capacity as Auden's secretary, an interesting writer; after we met at a table outside a Plaka Kafeneion, he allowed Gregory Corso to invite me on the spur of the moment to his house in Kolonaki for lunch the next day, back during my first trip to Greece, in 1966 I think it was—the only time I ever saw him. (How would we get through these one-sentence restrictions without the semicolon?) In his kitchen I ate Gregory's very hot rice, peppers, and sausage concoction ("Aw, man—you guys don't have to eat this shit," was his own verdict on what he'd made, but Ansen and I both did;

I had come in a tie, slacks, and sports jacket: Greg was in jeans and some kind of short-sleeved shirt); and there were original Cocteau drawings framed and hung on the walls, I remember. I only saw him on two consecutive afternoons, both times with Corso, whom I only ran into about five times—four times in Greece, and once a few years later in the Lower East Side.

Later, I remember learning that his home was where Chester Kallman was staying when, years later, he drank himself to death once his older partner, Auden, had passed away.

George Eliot was a great English novelist whom C.L.R. James ranked with Melville, when James was writing *Mariners, Renegades & Castaways*. *Moby-Dick* and *Middlemarch* were his two nominees for the great mid-nineteenth-century English-language masterpieces. I can't argue.

Junot Díaz: an extremely hardworking writer, who puts immense amounts of effort into the Pulitzer work he does on the prize committee every year, and his own political work, as well as his own writing, of which there is far too little, though what there is is beautiful and exquisitely crafted: *Drown* is an amazing book, and the concluding novella, "Negocios," took my head off when I first read it; it still holds up well. And I'll say the same for his novel *The Brief Wondrous Life of Oscar Wao*. He is also a wondrously patient and loyal friend to an often confused older fellow.

You often speak of writing as "discourse." With yourself? With the reader? Is it the same for fiction and nonfiction?

I'm using "discourse" in an older sense: discourse as response, understanding, discourse as structure both conscious and unconscious: not dialogue, but what impels and structures dialogue: not the "discourse between . . ." but the "discourse of . . ."

My son (formerly of Tenth and A) tells me that hipsters are moving back to the Lower East Side because it's more affordable than Brooklyn. Is this a good thing?

My understanding of the mysteries of gentrification or of what happens inside or around it is just not that great. I don't know the neighborhood anymore, nor have I been there for years. We'll let that one sit.

You had a long relationship with the late, lamented David Hartwell, SF's Maxwell Perkins. How did that come about?

It began as the friendship between two young men who both liked Science Fiction, both liked poetry, both liked music. David was a year my senior, and in the first years I knew him, he did get his PhD and worked very hard on a poetry magazine called *The Little Magazine*, of whose voluntary staff I was a member. How we actually met I don't recall, but I believe it revolved around Paul Williams, creator of an extremely successful music fanzine that became the first serious rock 'n' roll magazine, which I got to write for, named *Crawdaddy*. At the time, Paul was going with Trina Robbins, who was about five or six years older than he was, and was then a dress designer. She made Marilyn's dress that she wore to the Nebula Awards (which I attended not only with an unhappy Marilyn—she'd only agreed to come because I assured her I hadn't won—but with my mother and sister and an albino friend named Whit Whitman, who came in a black denim suit, and with whom I had been to bed a couple of times and was a friend of Marilyn's from the Old Reliable, while I wore a black tuxedo and a silver lamé turtleneck), the night Fred delivered his jeremiad—and I won my second and third Nebula Awards (a total surprise to me) in one evening.

Even after *Nova* was written, I was still not sure if I was going to be a musician or a writer. David was often my best friend and on more than one occasion saved my ass. But the absurdity of trying to capture a long friendship in a paragraph . . . What can I say? I'm glad it happened and I miss that I'll never get to go out to lunch with him again, down near where he worked at Tor Books, in the Fuller Building (better known as the Flatiron) on Twenty-Third and Fifth. The history of science fiction tends to be the history of its editors, and David was the most important of those editors since the crop in the 1950s, Campbell, Gold, Boucher, Cele Goldsmith, and the Furmans, Joe and Ed.

I was lucky to be as close to him as I was. At his death, we had physically drifted apart, even as we'd come to appreciate and respect each other—at least on my side—more and more. His sudden and unexpected death startled us all. There were a lot of young editors, both at Tor and at other places, whom he'd trained. We'll see what kind of job they do.

After all, he was the editor who pretty much discovered you, wasn't he?

Yes, he was—and I'm glad I got (and took) the chance to thank him for my career that time we were all at Williams College together. The last time I saw him. But enough about me. What's next for Samuel R. Delany?

Probably I need to get some lunch, which is about as far ahead as I can see right now. I hope some of this was of interest. But we all live our lives from the inside of our bodies out, not from the outside in. Which is why fiction has the texture that it does.

Thanks for the questions, Terry.

Bibliography

FICTION

The Jewels of Aptor (1962)

The Fall of the Towers trilogy:
Out of the Dead City (1963)
The Towers of Toron (1964)
City of a Thousand Suns (1965)

The Ballad of Beta-2 (1965)
Babel-17 (1966)
Empire Star (1966)
The Einstein Intersection (1967)
Nova (1968)
Driftglass (1969)
Equinox (1973)
Dhalgren (1975)
Trouble on Triton (1976)

Return to Nevèrÿon series:
Tales of Nevèrÿon (1979)
Neveryóna (1982)
Flight from Nevèrÿon (1985)
Return to Nevèrÿon (1987)

Distant Stars (1981)
Stars in My Pocket Like Grains of Sand (1984)
Driftglass/Starshards (collected stories, 1993)
They Fly at Çiron (1993)
The Mad Man (1994)
Hogg (1995)
Atlantis: Three Tales (1995)
Aye, and Gomorrah (2004)
Phallos (2004)
Dark Reflections (2007)
Through the Valley of the Nest of Spiders (2012)
A, B, C: Three Short Novels (2015)

GRAPHIC NOVELS

Empire (artist, Howard Chaynkin, 1980)
Bread & Wine (artist, Mia Wolff, 1999)

NONFICTION

The Jewel-Hinged Jaw (1977; revised, 2008)
The American Shore (1978)
Heavenly Breakfast (1979)

Starboard Wine (1984; revised, 2008)

The Motion of Light in Water (1988)

Wagner/Artaud (1988)

The Straits of Messina (1990)

Silent Interviews (1994)

Longer Views (1996)

Times Square Red, Times Square Blue (1999)

Shorter Views (1999)

1984: Selected Letters (2000)

About Writing (2005)

In Search of Silence: The Journals of Samuel R. Delany: Volume 1, 1957–1968, ed. Kenneth R. James (2017)

About the Author

SAMUEL R. DELANY'S SCIENCE fiction and fantasy tales are available in *Aye and Gomorrah and Other Stories*. His collection *Atlantis: Three Tales* and *Phallos* are experimental fiction. His novels include science fiction such as the Nebula Award–winning *Babel-17* and *The Einstein Intersection*, as well as *Nova* and *Dhalgren*. His four-volume series Return to Nevèrÿon is sword-and-sorcery. Most recently, he has written the SF novel *Through the Valley of the Nest of Spiders*. His 2007 novel *Dark Reflections* won the Stonewall Book Award. Other novels include *Equinox, Hogg,* and *The Mad Man*. Delany was the subject of a 2007 documentary, *The Polymath,* by Fred Barney Taylor, and he has written a popular creative writing textbook, *About Writing*. He is the author of the widely taught *Times Square Red / Times Square Blue* and has written a Hugo Award–winning autobiography, *The Motion of Light in Water*. All are available as both e-books and in paperback.

Delany is the author of several collections of critical essays.

His interview in the *Paris Review*'s "Art of Fiction" series appeared in spring 2012. In 2013 he was made the 31st Damon Knight Memorial Grand Master of Science Fiction. In 2015 he was the recipient of the Nicolas Guillén Award for philosophical fiction. He lives in Philadelphia with his partner, Dennis Rickett.

Also available from PM Press

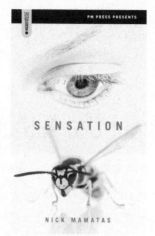

Sensation
NICK MAMATAS
ISBN: 978-1-60486-354-3
$14.95

Damnificados
JJ AMAWORO WILSON
ISBN: 978-1-62963-117-2
$15.95

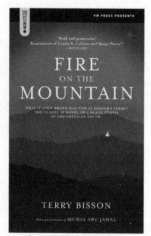

Fire on the Mountain
TERRY BISSON
Introduction by Mumia Abu-Jamal
ISBN: 978-1-60486-087-0
$15.95

Clandestine Occupations: An Imaginary History
DIANA BLOCK
ISBN: 978-1-62963-121-9
$16.95

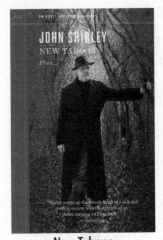
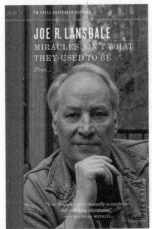

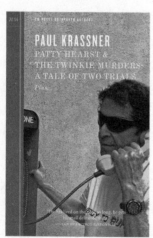
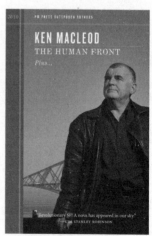

FRIENDS OF

These are indisputably momentous times—the financial system is melting down globally and the Empire is stumbling. Now more than ever there is a vital need for radical ideas.

In the years since its founding—and on a mere shoestring—PM Press has risen to the formidable challenge of publishing and distributing knowledge and entertainment for the struggles ahead. With hundreds of releases to date, we have published an impressive and stimulating array of literature, art, music, politics, and culture. Using every available medium, we've succeeded in connecting those hungry for ideas and information to those putting them into practice.

Friends of PM allows you to directly help impact, amplify, and revitalize the discourse and actions of radical writers, filmmakers, and artists. It provides us with a stable foundation from which we can build upon our early successes and provides a much-needed subsidy for the materials that can't necessarily pay their own way. You can help make that happen—and receive every new title automatically delivered to your door once a month—by joining as a Friend of PM Press. And, we'll throw in a free T-shirt when you sign up.

Here are your options:

- **$30 a month**: Get all books and pamphlets plus 50% discount on all webstore purchases
- **$40 a month**: Get all PM Press releases (including CDs and DVDs) plus 50% discount on all webstore purchases
- **$100 a month**: Superstar—Everything plus PM merchandise, free downloads, and 50% discount on all webstore purchases

For those who can't afford $30 or more a month, we have Sustainer Rates at $15, $10, and $5. Sustainers get a free PM Press T-shirt and a 50% discount on all purchases from our website.

Your Visa or Mastercard will be billed once a month, until you tell us to stop. Or until our efforts succeed in bringing the revolution around. Or the financial meltdown of Capital makes plastic redundant. Whichever comes first.

PM Press was founded at the end of 2007 by a small collection of folks with decades of publishing, media, and organizing experience. PM Press co-conspirators have published and distributed hundreds of books, pamphlets, CDs, and DVDs. Members of PM have founded enduring book fairs, spearheaded victorious tenant organizing campaigns, and worked closely with bookstores, academic conferences, and even rock bands to deliver political and challenging ideas to all walks of life. We're old enough to know what we're doing and young enough to know what's at stake.

We seek to create radical and stimulating fiction and nonfiction books, pamphlets, T-shirts, visual and audio materials to entertain, educate, and inspire you. We aim to distribute these through every available channel with every available technology—whether that means you are seeing anarchist classics at our bookfair stalls; reading our latest vegan cookbook at the café; downloading geeky fiction e-books; or digging new music and timely videos from our website.

PM Press is always on the lookout for talented and skilled volunteers, artists, activists, and writers to work with. If you have a great idea for a project or can contribute in some way, please get in touch.

PM Press
PO Box 23912
Oakland CA 94623
510-658-3906
www.pmpress.org